Baby-sitters'
European Vacation

Other books by
Ann M. Martin

Baby-sitters'
European Vacation

Ann M. Martin

An
APPLE
PAPERBACK

SCHOLASTIC INC.
New York Toronto London Auckland Sydney

*The author gratefully acknowledges
Peter Lerangis
for his help in
preparing this manuscript.*

Cover art by Hodges Soileau

Interior art by Angelo Tillery

ISBN 0-590-06000-7

12 11 10 9 8 7 6 5 4 3 2   8 9/9 0 1 2 3/0

Printed in the U.S.A.   40

First Scholastic printing, July 1998

PROLOGUE

BSC European Journal
Jessi Ramsey Version
The Prequel

          Saturday

Dear Mary Anne,
Dawn, and Claudia,
   I know, I
shouldn't be writing
in this yet.
   It's a travel
journal. We're all
still in Stoneybrook
   Besides, we'll
be seeing each
other at Kristy's
big farewell party
tonight.
   But I have to
write. Otherwise I
may float away.

I have been
dancing all day
long. Screaming,
too. I pack an
outfit. Then I
let out a scream.
Then I pack some
more.

I have never
been out of this
country in my
whole life. And
tomorrow I,
Jessica Ramsey,
am flying to
Europe!

Oops. Screamed
again.

Aunt Cecelia
is mad at me.
She says I'm
making Becca
jealous.

Frankly I
think Becca will
survive just
fine. She's
already practicing
for her European

trip when she's in sixth grade.

(She's convinced that Stoneybrook Middle School will arrange the exact same tour three years from now.)

So she's speaking with a British accent. She even tape-recorded Victoria Kent (before Vicki went home to London, just to pick up slang. Like "abfab. As in "_absolutely fabulous_." (Squirt loves hearing that He says "Fabab!")

Is this ironic or what? Considering Vicki had been trying desperately to sound 100% American.

I can just picture it — the English princess bouncing around her castle saying "way cool" to all her courtiers, while Becca's making a scene at the Washington Mall, shouting "abfab," and "top hole" and "quite right."

Well, maybe not. Today Becca finally realized I'm going to France too, not just England. So she's watching a lot of Pepe LePew cartoons.

Now she has a new expression. All day long she's been saying, "Ooh-la-laaaa...."

CHAPTER 1

Jessi

*The Prequel
Part Two*

Still Saturday.
Still here.
But already my
trip has changed.
I had the best
news today . . . .

Jessi

"**Y**ou're *what?*" Maritza Cruz's voice snapped at me over the telephone.

She was mad. I could tell. I mean, I hadn't spoken to her in weeks, and suddenly, the day before my flight, I was calling to say I was off to Europe.

Maritza lives in Brooklyn, New York. She and I were in a month-long program for promising dancers in NYC, working with the ballet company Dance New York. We grew so-o-o-o close during that month. Almost like sisters.

Some sister I was. Long-lost.

"I know. I'm sorry," I replied. "My school offered this trip really late, and you had to sign up, but the spaces were limited, so I wasn't exactly sure I'd be going. And we had to have all these meetings, and this Canadian school is taking the trip with us, so we had to learn about —"

"Where in Europe?" Maritza interrupted.

"England, France . . ."

"London?"

"Yeah. And Paris —"

"AAAAAAAAUUUUGGGGHHHHH!"

I had to take the receiver from my ear. "I promise I'll write —"

"No. That's not it. Tanisha's going to be there! The whole Dance New York company is performing there!"

6

"AAAAAAAAUUUUGGGGHHHHH!" Now it was my turn to shriek. I could not believe it. *My* dance company — the group I trained with, the group I was invited to join — was going to be with me on my vacation!

Okay, let me explain. First of all, Tanisha is Maritza's older sister. Tanisha is a member of the "permanent company," personally selected by the head of Dance NY, David Brailsford. (Yes, *the* David Brailsford, ballet legend, and yes, he did ask me to join. And I still may someday. I'm only eleven, so I have time.) Anyway, if you're in the company, Dance NY *is* your school. You take intensive dance classes in the company's studios in Manhattan, you study your academic subjects with tutors, and you travel all over the world.

"You *have* to go see them, Jessi!" Maritza said. "They're playing at a place called the Barbican. And guess what they're performing? *Gotham Rhythm.*"

"Oh."

Pssshhhh went my excitement. Like air out of a bicycle tire.

I *knew Gotham Rhythm.* Maritza and I had learned it during our training. We had performed it at a recital.

Which means that if I *had* joined the permanent company, I would have been going to Europe with them. I would have been *performing* instead of watching.

I did not want to think about that. I was in too good a mood.

But boy, it was hard to sound cheerful.

I gave Maritza the name of the hotel I'd be staying in. She promised she'd talk to Tanisha.

After I hung up, my brain was going a mile a minute.

You said no for a good reason, Jessi, it told me.

Which is true. I mean, I *could* have said yes to Mr. Brailsford if I lived in New York City. But Stoneybrook is two hours away, so I'd have had to commute to school. Or move.

I was frustrated at first, but I took it in stride. Frankly, I couldn't stand the idea of leaving all my Stoneybrook friends anyway.

I mean, I do love Maritza and my other Dance NY friends. But Stoneybrook is my home. I belong here.

I haven't always felt that way. I *hated* Stoneybrook when I first moved here. Some of our neighbors were awful to my family. They obviously didn't want African-Americans in their neighborhood. I was dying to move back to my hometown, Oakley, New Jersey, which was much more racially mixed.

Things are better now. People grow up, I

guess. Attitudes change. And I don't miss Oakley as much anymore.

What really glues me to Stoneybrook is the Baby-sitters Club. My absolute best friends.

Which one is the absolutest? Mallory Pike. We are like sisters. We practically read each other's minds. Which is pretty funny, considering how different we seem on the surface. For one thing, Mal has pale, freckly skin and reddish-brown hair. She doesn't dance at all, and she's obsessed with creative writing and illustrating. Plus she has a huge, unruly family that includes *eight* kids — and cousins all over the globe. (Well, at least in England. She was planning to visit them during our trip.) The very ruly Ramseys, on the other hand, all live in the States, as far as I know, and our branch has only three kids (me, Becca, and my baby brother, Squirt).

What do Mal and I have in common? Well, each of us is the oldest child in the family. That means our parents expect us to be perfect but treat us like babies. (If you're an eldest sib, you know what I mean. The younger ones have it *so* much easier.) But the main thing we share is *passion*. We do things in a big way. Mal is as dedicated to writing as I am to dancing. Also, we both love horses and horse books, and we have read just about every one ever written.

9

Jessi

But most of all, we are passionate about baby-sitting. You have to feel that way to be part of the Baby-sitters Club.

Mal and I are junior officers. We're the only sixth-graders among thirteen-year-old eighth-graders, so it's kind of an honor to be included. Not that anyone ever says that. We treat each other as equals. Mal and I do everything the other members do — well, except baby-sit away from home at night. But that's only because our parents won't allow us to. (I told you they treat us like babies.)

The basic idea of the BSC?

A. Gather a group of reliable sitters at one phone number.

B. Make yourselves available during convenient hours for booking jobs (in our case, Mondays, Wednesdays, and Fridays from five-thirty until six).

C. Let local parents know about the group.

D. Wait for the job offers to pour in.

Simple, huh? Parents have one-stop shopping, sitters have regular work (plus an excuse for best friends to hang out together three times a week), and everybody's happy.

Who's the genius behind this idea? Picture a short, athletic-looking Caucasian seventh-grader who can't sit still. She has brown eyes and shoulder-length brown hair, and she's dressed in jeans and a sweatshirt. Ta-da: Kristy Thomas. Now imagine her living in a little house with three brothers (two older and one younger) and a mom who is single because Kristy's dad skipped out on the family. Now picture Kristy watching her mom call frantically around town in search of a sitter for Kristy's youngest brother, David Michael. An idea is forming. . . .

Cut to the present. Kristy now lives in a mansion, because her mom got married again, to a guy named Watson Brewer, who happens to be rich. Home life is just the way Kristy likes it, which is total chaos. At her house live not only her three brothers, but two stepsiblings, an adopted sister, and a live-in grandmother. And Kristy is now the president of a super-successful baby-sitting organization. In addition to seven regular members, it includes two associates who help out in emergencies, and even one honorary member. (More about them later.)

Zoom in on BSC headquarters, also known as the bedroom of Claudia Kishi. Kristy is bossing everyone around, in her loud voice. Claudia, the club vice-president, is burrowing under her bed, pushing aside piles of old sketches, paintings, and beads.

For Claudia, imagine a trim Japanese-

11

American girl with long hair and beautiful skin, wearing some cool outfit she's put together from thrift shop and vintage clothing store finds.

Claudia has two main talents: art and junk food. The art is obvious. You can see her paintings on the walls, a new project on her easel, and her homemade jewelry around our wrists and necks.

The junk food is hidden. Her parents don't mind Creativity, but they frown on Bad Nutrition.

As Claudia emerges with a bag of Kit-Kats, she nearly collides with a blonde girl in a cutting-edge black ensemble. That's Claudia's best friend, Stacey McGill. Her fashion sense practically screams "New York City!" She is lucky enough to have been born and raised there, and she still visits regularly, to see her divorced dad. Stacey's our treasurer and resident math whiz. In this scene she's collecting dues money from all the members (which, by the way, happens only on Mondays).

You may notice that Stacey is the only one not accepting a Kit-Kat from Claudia's bag. That's because she has diabetes, which means her body cannot handle refined sugars. If she eats too much sugar — or too little — she could become very sick. But as long as she has regular meals, stays away from sweets, and gives herself daily injections of insulin, she leads a perfectly normal life. (I know, *ew,* right? That's what I used to think, but Stacey insists it's no big deal.)

Luckily Claudia has chips too, which Stacey *can* eat. And does.

So now you're seeing us in our typical state — pigging out — when suddenly the phone rings.

Abby Stevenson snatches up the receiver. (No, she's not the *only* member who answers the phone. We all can.) As she holds it to her ear, it disappears under her lion's-mane of curly hair. She says something like, "Baby-sitters Club, no job too small, no kid too big!" because she's . . . well, *Abby.* Dedicated to the art of saying weird things and making people laugh.

Abby's our alternate officer. That means she takes over for any absent officer. She's also our newest member. She moved from Long Island (with her mom and twin sister, Anna) to a house up the street from Kristy not long after our former alternate officer, Dawn Schafer, moved away. Just in time too, because we were swamped with job offers. We asked both sisters to join the BSC, but Anna turned us down. She's a budding concert violinist, and she practices during prime baby-sitting hours.

Abby is very different from her quiet, thoughtful sister. Abby's loud and funny. She's super-

13

athletic. She's asthmatic too, which means she has to carry around a prescription inhaler. And she has about a million allergies — pollen, strawberries, dogs, kitty litter, dust, you name it.

Sometimes it's hard to imagine Abby being serious about anything. But she is, deep down. I see her serious side whenever she talks about her dad, who died in a car crash a few years ago. I also saw that side of her in synagogue. Abby and Anna invited all of us BSC members to their Bat Mitzvah, a ceremony that marks the passage into womanhood for Jewish girls. The twins had to recite in Hebrew, and they did it beautifully.

Anyway, back to the scene at Claudia's. The phone call is a job request from a client. Abby is taking down the info, and she promises to call back. As she hangs up, we all turn to Mary Anne Spier.

Think neat and shy, preppyish clothes, warm brown eyes, short brown hair. That's Mary Anne. As secretary, she's in charge of the BSC record book, which contains our job calendar. With one glance, Mary Anne immediately knows who's available. The calendar dates are neatly marked with all our jobs *and* our conflicts — medical appointments, after-school activities, family getaways, and so on. (In the back of the book is a client list: addresses, phone numbers, rates charged, and notes about the kids we baby-sit for.)

Shy, modest Mary Anne and loud, opinionated Kristy have been best friends since birth. They used to live across the street from each other. (If you drew a line connecting their old houses and Claudia's, you'd make a triangle.) But first Kristy moved to another house in Stoneybrook, and then so did Mary Anne, after her dad married Sharon Schafer.

Recognize the name? Sharon is Dawn Schafer's mom. Richard and Sharon were once high school sweethearts, until fate separated them. Off they went to separate colleges, and eventually marriages and their own families. But Richard didn't have it easy. Mrs. Spier died shortly after Mary Anne was born. While he recovered from the grief, he let his parents-in-law raise Mary Anne. But when he tried to retrieve her, they refused. They thought he couldn't handle single parenthood. Well, he *did* finally get Mary Anne back, but he went overboard to prove himself. He raised Mary Anne super-strictly — rules, rules, rules. (She had to wear pigtails and little-girl outfits right up to seventh grade!) When he finally started easing up on her, fate stepped in again: In California, Sharon had divorced her husband. She moved back to

15

Jessi

her hometown, Stoneybrook (with Dawn and Dawn's brother, Jeff). And the rest is legend: (1) *The Joining:* Dawn is accepted into the BSC, (2) *The Discovery:* Dawn and Mary Anne find out about the long-lost love, (3) *The Matchmaking:* They bring together the lovebirds, and (4) *A New Family:* After a big wedding, Mary Anne and Dawn become stepsisters!

Now, *that's* a happy ending.

Well, sort of. Jeff moved back to California. After awhile, so did Dawn, which devastated Mary Anne.

But they talk on the phone all the time. And Dawn does visit a lot. (She's the honorary member I mentioned.)

This summer, for example, Dawn was in Stoneybrook. She, Claudia, Mary Anne, and Logan Bruno (Mary Anne's boyfriend) had been selected to be counselors at the Playground Camp run by Stoneybrook Elementary School.

By the way, Dawn is in our BSC scene too. She has blue eyes and light blonde (almost white) hair that hangs down to her waist. She's wearing bell-bottoms and a loose-fitting top. And she's probably munching on some disgusting health food snack, like turnip chips.

Logan is *not* in the scene (which is just as well, because he would tease Dawn about her cuisine). Neither is Shannon Kilbourne, an eighth-

Jessi

grader who goes to a private school called Stoneybrook Day School. They are our associate members, and they're not required to attend meetings or pay dues.

Now you have a picture of all my best friends.

Add thirty minutes of phone calls, laughter, and eating, and you have a good idea of why I didn't want to move to New York City.

My fame and fortune can wait. Traveling to Europe with my best friends is something I'd never want to miss.

I opened my dresser drawer, pulled out a leotard and some ballet slippers, and tucked them into my suitcase.

If I was going to meet the Dance NY kids and see Mr. Brailsford, I'd better stay in shape.

A few hours of practice in hotel rooms wouldn't hurt.

CHAPTER 2

Abby

Today, Stoneybrook.
Tomorrow, Abby's new
life begins.

Checklist for Meeting
the Queen
   1. Avoid scaring
her: brush hair.
   2. Check between
teeth for unsightly
bits of lunch.
   3. De-gooberize
nose in advance.
   4. Shake hands
gently to avoid
breaking elderly
fingers.

5. Do not kiss her on lips.

6. Ask about Elvis only if the opportunity presents itself....

Abby

"*E*lvis? Abby, please." Kristy Thomas rolled her eyes at me, then turned toward the buffet table.

"He *must* have performed in Europe," I said, munching on some carrot sticks. "He was an international star. Like the Queen. I'll bet she met him."

The BSC going-away party was in full swing. We were all crowded around the grub table. Watson and Kristy's mom had made a lot of the food themselves.

The music? Well, it was Watson-esque — old-fashioned big-band vinyl records. We tolerated it because the food was good.

I was dying to sneak around in his record library and find some vintage Elvis recordings.

I LUV Elvis (surprised, huh?). I don't know why I do. I just always have. I've been to his house, Graceland, with some other BSC members. It was definitely one of the cooler experiences of my life.

"First of all, your list makes no sense," Kristy said. "I mean, who says we're going to meet the Queen?"

"Just in case," I replied. "We *are* visiting Victoria's castle, right? Maybe the Queen'll drop by to borrow some sugar."

"Yuck," exclaimed Dawn Schafer, Duchess of Health, as she loaded sprouts onto her plate.

"Actually, I don't think Victoria really lives in a castle," said Mary Anne. "She does like to exaggerate."

Claudia nodded, her mouth full. "Ishpobbiapashashum."

"Swallow, please," Stacey said.

"It's probably just a palace or something," Claudia repeated.

"Anyway, Elvis was in the army," I said, "so he might have entertained the overseas troops during the war. But where?"

Claudia spun around from the table, her plate stacked high with tortilla chips and pretzels. "Elvis was in a war? Which one?"

"I don't know," I admitted. "Civil?"

Kristy nearly spat out her Triscuits. "That was in the eighteen hundreds. Didn't they teach you that on Long Island?"

I shrugged. "I must have been absent that day."

"Maybe he sang at the Barbican," Jessi suggested. "That's where I'm seeing Dance New York."

"Cool," Stacey remarked. "Can you get us tickets?"

"Not me," Kristy said. "I'll be busy visiting all the cricket stadiums."

"Are those like flea markets?" I asked.

Kristy threw a dinner roll at me.

"You're all crazy," Claudia grumbled. "I'm glad I decided to stay."

She put her arm around Mary Anne. But Mary Anne didn't look too happy.

In fact, she was on the verge of tears.

Jessi smiled at her sympathetically. "We're going to miss you too, Mary Anne."

Fwoosh. Up went the floodgates.

Logan Bruno was the first to hug Mary Anne. Then Kristy. Then the rest of us.

A big old BSC group hug.

A weepy one.

"Who died?" asked Sam Thomas, Kristy's fifteen-year-old brother.

"Can't you let us have a Moment?" I asked.

Mary Anne was wiping away sniffles. "I'm really glad I signed up for Playground Camp. But I don't know. . . . I guess it's hard seeing you so excited. And knowing I'll be here . . ."

"Hey, a choice is a choice," Logan remarked.

"Thank you, O Wise One," I said.

Stacey sighed. "Not all of us are so thrilled about the trip, Mary Anne."

"Right," Kristy agreed. "We have to share it with this strange school. Who knows what those kids'll be like?"

"That's not it," Stacey murmured.

"Don't tell me," Claudia said. "Harrods is closed for renovations. You won't be able to shop."

"I'll be shopping," Stacey replied. "But I'll be with Mom. And possibly Robert."

Robert is Stacey's former boyfriend. Mom is Stacey's permanent mother.

Personally, I think they're both pretty cool. But I'm not Stacey.

"Hey, your mom's not the only chaperone," I reminded her. "When we split into groups, go with Mr. Dougherty or a chaperone from that Canadian school."

"Right," Stacey muttered. "Abby, you don't *know* my mom. She used to lead me around New York City with a telephone cord attached to my waist!"

Claudia nodded solemnly. "But she gave that up when you turned thirteen."

"Don't worry," Dawn reassured her. "I thought Jeff would ruin my family trip, but I didn't even notice he was there. There's just so much to see."

"You went to England?" Kristy asked.

"No. France." Dawn's eyes grew faraway and misty. "The Loire Valley. . . . I still remember the names of the chateaux: Chambord, Chenonceaux, Chervery, Chinon —"

"Champagne?" asked Watson, holding out a tray of drinks.

"That was beautiful too," Dawn said.

"The *drink*, Dawn," Kristy said. "Not the *region*."

Actually, it wasn't champagne. Watson was offering us sparkling apple cider. Which, in my opinion, tastes much better.

We each took one beautiful, fluted glass. And Mrs. Brewer announced, "I want to propose a toast. Here's to a safe, educational trip!"

"A *fun* trip!" Kristy called out.

"To adventure!" Mallory piped up.

"To shopping!" Stacey said.

"To Mary Anne, Claudia, and Dawn!" Jessi said.

Logan held up his hand. "Uh, hello?"

"And Logan too," Mary Anne said.

"To a break from baby-sitting!" I added.

"Yyyyyes!"

I don't know who yelled that.

But we all drank to it.

Stacey

Sunday

We're off !
Au revoir, États-Unis !
Ta-ta, Yanks !
We are now passing the curvy
arm of Cape Cod, Massachusetts.
Below us is nothing but ocean.
The next land we see will be...
the Old Country !

Stacey

What a weird expression.

That's what Mr. Dougherty had been saying since we'd arrived at the airport. "Next stop, the Old Country!"

When you think of it, though, it makes no sense. Europe isn't "older" than any other part of the world. I mean, dinosaurs lived in the Americas too.

Oh, well. I guess that's why Mr. Dougherty teaches creative writing, not science.

As our plane rose higher over the Atlantic, I could see Mr. D deep in conference with Mallory and a couple of other kids, giving them advice about their personal journals. He was probably telling them to seek out places where the famous writers hung out. Shakespeare's favorite snack shop. Whatever.

He was wearing a beret. I think that is *so* corny. I remember the time Dad bought one, way back when our family went to Ireland. He thought it looked cosmopolitan. Mom thought it looked dorky. So it stayed in his suitcase.

Fortunately, Mom was being very kind to Mr. D. She hadn't mentioned a thing about the beret. Nor about the stray pieces of honey-roasted peanut that were nesting in his big handlebar mustache.

Unlike everyone else in our group, I never received a bag of those peanuts. Mom had grilled the flight attendant about the sugar content, and then she made a scene, pointing me out and demanding that I be given a nonsugary snack.

As if I couldn't have taken care of that myself. Without making *everyone* in the cabin stare at me.

Grrrr.

Do I sound like a horrible daughter? I'm not. I love my mom. Because I'm an only child, and Mom's divorced, we're super-close. But in a way, that's the problem. Sometimes — just sometimes — it's nice to have a break.

I was sitting, by the way, in seat 29A. Mom was sitting in seat 14C.

I think Mom had imagined she'd be in seat 29B, next to me. The separate seating wasn't my fault. As I approached the ticket counter, Mom was off fetching kids from the candy shop (including Alan Gray, the Plague of the Eighth Grade, who should have been banned from the flight because he is definitely hazardous waste).

Well, maybe I did slide closer to the counter just then. I didn't exactly *wait* for Mom.

Anyway, Robert was standing next to me at the time, so the agent assigned us seats together.

I felt a little funny about that. Uncomfortable. I was hoping I'd be closer to Kristy, Abby, Jessi, and Mal.

27

Now, sitting in the plane, I could hear their voices, chattering away happily, while I sat silently next to my former boyfriend.

I mean, I *like* Robert. He's a great guy. Funny and kind and handsome. We had fun times back when we were going out. But that was so long ago. Phase One of our complicated relationship.

In Phase Two, we broke up.

In Phase Three, we made up and agreed to be just friends.

In Phase Four, Robert became needy and sad and depressed all the time. And he started treating me as if I were his girlfriend/best friend/mother/shrink all rolled into one.

In Phase Five, we talked it out. He seemed to understand how I felt: that *I* needed a little breathing room and *he* needed to lean on other people, not just me.

Robert got the message. He began having some long talks with his baseball coach, who really seemed to help. Over the early summer, Robert and I hadn't seen much of each other. Not that we'd been avoiding contact. We just finally became real, honest-to-goodness *friends*.

I liked it that way. A little distance was just what we needed.

So I was feeling nervous on the plane. I was worried I'd given him the wrong signal at the airport counter. Did he think I'd *plotted* to sit next to him?

"This is way cool," Robert exclaimed. "It's too bad we can't see outside." (We were taking a night flight, so we'd have a full day ahead of us when we arrived in London.)

"Don't tell me this is your first plane ride," I said.

"First one overseas," he replied.

"Uh-huh. Wow."

I needed to loosen up. I was tense.

I took a deep breath. My brain started putting together a conversation.

I turned toward Robert. He was facing away from me. Looking at a pair of extremely tight bell-bottoms.

Well, at the girl *in* the bell-bottoms. Jacqui Grant.

"Are you going to finish those?" Jacqui asked sweetly, nodding toward his bag of honey-roasted peanuts. Which was *obviously* empty.

"These?" Robert held up the bag. "Sorry."

Jacqui giggled. "I am *such* a pig."

Robert smiled shyly.

"Isn't this the *clearest* day?" Now Jacqui was standing in the aisle, leaning over Robert.

Way over Robert. With a low-cut shirt that showed . . . well, a lot.

Puh-leeze. I mean, how obvious can you get?

This was no accident. I know Jacqui pretty well. We used to hang out together. She got me into big trouble once at a rock concert. She sneaked liquor into the stadium and was caught — and she blamed me. I have never, ever forgotten that.

Jacqui has tried to flirt with Robert before, but it didn't work. She's not his type. He doesn't go for girls with red-and-green-dyed hair and nose rings.

"You can really see *so much*, Jacqui," I said.

Not that I cared.

I was just annoyed at Jacqui's obnoxiousness. That's all.

Jacqui finally gave up when the captain turned on the FASTEN SEAT BELT sign. By that time the meal was about to be served.

Not much to tell about the rest of the flight. The airline's diabetic meal was a salad that tasted as if it had earned frequent flyer miles for life. The in-flight movie put me to sleep. Which was good, since we were flying through the middle of the night. Eventually I did have a chance to walk around the cabin and visit my friends. Of course, Jacqui moved right in on Robert. And she wasn't the only one. At one point she was sitting in my seat while Kathleen Lopez *and* Kara Mauricio were facing him from the seats in front.

How did I feel about this? A little strange, I have to admit. But hey, it's a free country. And it was good to see him talking to someone besides me.

When we started our descent into London, the plane began bucking. You couldn't see a thing out the windows. Just morning fog. The captain kept telling us that things were fine, and I tried to believe him.

But when those wheels hit the ground, my knuckles were white from grabbing the armrest.

When we finally stepped onto solid land, I was so relieved.

Now, I have done a fair amount of traveling, and most airports look the same. But the minute I stepped into Heathrow Airport, I wanted to scream with delight.

I don't know why. Maybe it was the relief. Or maybe the unfamiliar billboards. The accent of the airport announcer. The £ before all the prices on the ads.

It all just felt . . . so totally, fantastically foreign.

Jessi was twirling around on the tile floor. "Even the *air* smells different!"

"Tallyho!" Mr. Dougherty suddenly called out, marching toward the baggage claim area. "Once more into the breach!"

Nobody was paying much attention to him.

We were all yakking like crazy. Alan was trying to sneak off into a sweetshop. Abby and Kristy were reading billboards and laughing at the strange phrases.

It was only when things started to slow down a little that I realized how tired I was. After all, it was still the middle of the night in Stoneybrook!

Mom had to usher us all to the baggage area, which was total, absolute chaos.

At least one other flight was sharing our conveyor belt. People were blocking every inch of it, so we had to squeeze between them whenever we saw our suitcases. Little kids were screaming and running around, and Alan Gray actually stopped the carousel for a long time because he sat on it.

It seemed like hours before we retrieved everything, and *then* we had to wait in line for customs. By this time, I was *dying* for a nap.

"Are they going to search us?" Mallory asked.

"Oh, no," said Mr. Dougherty reassuringly. "It's just a formality. They only search the suspected terrorists."

Mr. D was one of the first ones through. Mom waited until the end, herding the rest of us. (I felt bad for her. Mr. D seemed to be in his own world.)

Mallory, Jessi, Kristy, Abby, and I didn't stop

jabbering. The customs officials just stamped our passports and waved us by.

As we dragged our luggage toward the exit, I heard a commotion. Mom's voice. Pleading.

I spun around.

"There must be some mistake," she was saying as she walked behind two customs officials, who were heading toward a small office.

Between them, looking very scared, was Alan Gray.

"Oh my lord . . ." I mumbled.

Kristy had a different reaction. I'll bet her laugh could have been heard halfway to Wales.

Well, guess why Alan was stopped. He had been acting suspicious on purpose — pretending to hide stuff in potted plants, tying a kerchief over his mouth, speaking in a nonsense language.

I figured the experience would quiet him down. But no. He was proud of himself. He said they had tortured him, tied him to a chair, shone flashlights in his eyes, and asked him about his connections to the Stoneybrook Liberation Front.

Alan Gray is such a jerk.

Fortunately he sat far from me on the bus to our hotel. The ride kind of freaked me out, even though I *knew* that the English drive on the *left* side of the road. It felt as if we were heading for an accident anyway. But I grew used to it. Before long my nose was plastered to the window, like everyone else's.

London is mega-cool. Crowded, narrow streets, a little like Greenwich Village in NYC, but with *much* older buildings. Even though we were all tired, our excitement jolted us awake.

As we came closer to our hotel, we passed an enormous park.

"Kensington Palace," Jessi read from a sign. "Can we stop in?"

"We're scheduled to take a tour later this week," Mom said.

"Maybe that's where Victoria Kent lives," Abby suggested.

"Oh? A member of the royal family?" asked Mr. Dougherty.

"Like, forty-ninth in line to the throne," I explained.

Mr. Dougherty laughed good-naturedly. "She's probably in one of the lower-priced palaces."

As the bus continued to wind through the streets, Mallory suddenly let out a gasp. "Baker Street!"

"Yeah, I could go for some pastries," Kristy said.

Mallory shook her head. "No! That's where Sherlock Holmes lived!"

"I knew that," Kristy muttered.

"And there's Marylebone Lane, where Charles Dickens wrote several of his books," Mr. Dougherty said.

"Kristy knew that too," Abby remarked.

Kristy stuck out her tongue.

Before long, we pulled up to our hotel, the Cardington Inn. It had begun to rain, so we raced to move our luggage out of the cargo hold on the bus and into the front lobby.

It wasn't at all what I expected. I guess I've seen too many *Fawlty Towers* reruns with Mom, so I had pictured a run-down place with eccentric characters running around.

The Cardington was as modern and comfy as a Holiday Inn.

Just inside, we were met by a balding man in a tweed jacket, smoking a pipe.

"The return of the colonists!" Mr. Dougherty announced, shaking the man's hand. "From New England to Old. I'm Dougherty, from the Stoneybrook Middle School."

"Phelps," replied the man. "From the Cotswolds."

Then, without another word, he walked out the front door.

Mr. Dougherty looked bewildered.

"He's a *guest*," Mom whispered.

We were cracking up. Poor Mr. Dougherty was bright red.

Mom quickly found the desk marked RECEP-
TION and spoke with a clerk.

"The other school has already arrived," she
announced to us. "Let's settle into our rooms,
and I'll find out when and where the two
groups are going to meet."

The clerk handed Mom a big envelope and
said, "Take the lift to the third story. And heavy
rain is on its way, so if you do go out, remember
your macs, wellies, and bumbershoots!"

As we piled onto the "lift" (which means
"elevator"), we were politely trying not to
laugh.

Except Alan Gray. *"Bumbershoots?"* he cried
out. "Sounds like some kind of weird veg-
etable."

"You have relatives here?" asked Kristy.

Ding! The lift opened on the third floor
(which was really the *fourth* floor, but the English count them differently). Mom was hand-
ing out room assignments. "Jessi and Mal:
three-oh-seven . . . Abby and Kara: three-ten . . .
Stacey and Kristy: three-twelve . . ."

I looked at Kristy. She looked at me. "Yyyes!"
we exclaimed at the same time.

My excitement lasted about two minutes.

It ended when I flipped my suitcase onto my
bed and opened it.

I recognized nothing inside. Tweed pants,

business shirts, argyle socks, boxer shorts — it was all *men's* stuff.

"Uh-oh," Kristy said, reaching for a metal canister tucked into the middle of the neatly piled clothing.

"Don't touch it!" I said. "It doesn't belong to —"

"What the heck is *this*?"

Kristy turned the canister around, revealing a label:

HANDLE WITH CARE

HUMAN ASHES

* * *

REMAINS OF

MR. D. PETROPOULOS

Kristy

Monday

Hi.

It's me. Kristy.

I shouldn't be writing this. But I have to. It's too weird.

Stacey just ran to find her mom, and they'll be back soon. So I don't have much time. Anyway, to make a long story short:

Stacey took the wrong suitcase at the airport. It looked exactly like hers. And when she opened it, she found the belongings of one guy — and the remains of another....

39

"What do you mean, *ashes*?" screamed Ms. McGill.

"Look!" Stacey grabbed the container and held it out.

I thought Ms. McGill was going to faint. *"Oh my lord. Stacey, do you know what that is?"*

"Yes! What am I going to do, Mom?"

"Put that thing down!"

"It's not a *thing*. It's a person."

"Put it down right this minute! And . . . and go wash your hands!"

Stacey dropped the canister. It's a good thing it landed in the suitcase, or Mr. D. Petropoulos would have been all over our hotel room floor.

I am so bad. I should not have been laughing. But I couldn't help it.

"It's not funny, Kristy," Stacey growled as she ran past me to the bathroom.

She was right. This was serious.

Morbid.

Tragic, really.

And not only for Stacey.

I mean, right that minute, some guy was opening up his suitcase, expecting to find his ash can — and pulling out designer dresses instead.

Just *thinking* about it made me laugh.

"I don't believe this is happening," Ms.

McGill said, pacing the room. "What do we do now?"

"I know." It was time to make myself useful. I went to the suitcase and flipped over the ID tag. "'Louis P. Anderson,'" I read. "'Forest Canyon Drive, Parker, Colorado.'"

"Let's contact the airline," Ms. McGill said, picking up the phone.

Stacey ran back into the room. "Wait! Doesn't this seem weird to you? I mean, why would this guy be carrying around someone else's ashes?"

"That's none of our business," Ms. McGill said.

"He might be . . . a smuggler or something," Stacey continued, a bit hysterically. "Or a serial killer. *And we have evidence.* If he finds out who we are, he could come after us."

"Stacey, you've been reading too many crime novels." Ms. McGill tapped out a number on the phone. "Our top priority is to get your luggage back."

"Let's head over to Baker Street and find Sherlock," I suggested.

I was just trying to lighten things up.

Neither Stacey nor Ms. McGill was amused.

"Yes, hello, I need the number for Interworld Airways," Ms. McGill said into the receiver.

Stacey sank into the bed. Her face was pale. "This is horrible. My whole vacation is ruined."

"I bet this kind of thing happens all the time," I said.

"Ashes in a suitcase?" Stacey shot back.

"No, lost luggage. We'll get it back."

"But I won't have anything to wear until then!"

"You can wear my clothes," I offered.

"Your —?" For a moment, Stacey looked as if I'd asked her to swim in a pool of spit. Then she forced a polite smile. "Thanks, but they're, um, probably too small."

I knew she'd say that.

I also knew the truth: Stacey would rather wear tinfoil than my kind of clothes. Outside of gym class, I do not believe a T-shirt or sweatpants have ever touched the skin of Anastasia McGill.

"We could go shopping right now," I said.

That idea seemed to cheer Stacey up.

"M-C-G-I-L-L," Ms. McGill spelled out to someone on the other end of the phone. "And I'm at the Cardington Inn. . . ."

She gave the phone number, said good-bye, and quickly hung up. "The good news," she said, "is that Mr. Anderson was probably on our flight, which means he may be staying somewhere in London. The airline will find out and leave a message at Reception. The bad news is that if we don't leave right now, we're going to

be late for our meeting with the kids from Ze-
hava Berger Junior High."

"But I can't go down there wearing *this*," said
Stacey.

"It's a beautiful, expensive outfit," Ms. McGill
protested.

"And it's been through a six-hour plane
ride!" Stacey exclaimed.

"Okay, I'll bring you something of mine," Ms.
McGill said, turning to leave.

"But — but —" Stacey sputtered.

Too late. Ms. McGill was gone.

Stacey looked as if she'd been sentenced to
death row. "I have to wear my *mom's* clothes?"

I eyed Mr. Anderson's suitcase. "You know,
Stace, some of those trousers look pretty nice."

I don't need to tell you Stacey's response to
that last comment.

She did, by the way, change into her mom's
skirt and sweater. The outfit looked fine to me,
but Stacey was mortified.

"What are people going to think?" she asked
as we stepped into the lift.

I shrugged. "That you're my mom?"

"Very funny, Kristy. Hilarious. I have stolen a
man's suitcase with a murder victim inside it,
the mob is about to close in, I'm making my European debut looking like a cover model for

Parenting magazine, *and you're making fun of me!*"

"You don't *know* he was murdered," I said.

Stacey wouldn't talk to me the rest of the way downstairs.

We were the last ones to reach the hotel meeting room. The Stoneybrook and Berger kids were huddled together — in two separate groups. Standing up. Ignoring each other.

It was kind of funny. But really immature.

At least Ms. McGill and Mr. D were mingling. They were off in a corner with the two Berger chaperones.

I could overhear some of the Berger kids speaking a foreign language. "French?" I asked Mallory.

She nodded. "Remember, they're from a Canadian school."

"I thought *Quebec* was the French-American city," Jessi remarked. "Toronto's in *Ontario*, right?"

"I guess Toronto has a few French speakers too," Mal said.

A silver-haired woman stepped forward and started clapping her hands. "Attention, please!" she said in a clipped British accent. "We're all here, so will everyone sit in a rough circle on the carpet?"

In a few minutes we were cross-legged on the

floor. The woman stood in the middle, next to a cute, young guy with wire-rimmed glasses and beard stubble. "I'm Ms. Post," the woman went on. "This is Mr. LaVigne. We work for the tour group, and we'll be your guides. Now, I know you and your chaperones have been flying all night and you're tired. We scheduled a light first day, and you may nap here if you like, but I do recommend you go to sleep later, on London time, even if your body tells you it's not time to do so. To begin our trip, I want us to get to know each other. So, will you all kindly take off one shoe and put it in a pile — Stoneybrook shoes to my right and Berger shoes to my left."

"A *shoe*?" Jessi whispered. "After we've been *in* them since yesterday?"

Abby grimaced. "Do they have oxygen masks handy?"

"When you're finished," Mr. LaVigne continued, "each of you will pick one shoe from the pile belonging to the other school. It will then be your responsibility to find the owner of the shoe and introduce him or her to your group."

Stacey buried her face in her hands. "Oh my lord. This is the most humiliating day of my entire life."

Personally, I thought the idea sounded cool. And I'd scribbled "Let's Go, Mets!" all over my sneakers, so that would be a real conversation starter. If my shoe happened to be picked by a baseball fan.

Soon two piles of shoes were in the center of the carpet. When Ms. Post said "Go," we all scrambled across the room, giggling.

I dived into the pile (I know, I get carried away). I came up with a guy's loafer, made of pretty fancy-looking soft black leather.

I looked inside for a name. Nothing.

All around me, kids were holding out shoes to one another. The whole thing seemed so silly. Everyone was howling with laughter.

"Whose shoe?" I called out, tossing the loafer up in the air a few times, so everyone could see it.

"Take it easy, that is imported glove leather!" a voice called out from behind me.

The accent was definitely French. I turned to face a guy with long black hair that draped across his left eye. He was wearing a loose-fitting shirt, like the kind pirates used to wear, only black.

"Hi," I said, extending my hand. "Kristy Thomas."

He took his shoe back before shaking my hand. "Michel DuMoulin."

"Michelle?" I asked.

He gave me a curious look. "You sound surprised."

46

"Well, it just — sounds like a girl's name. I mean, in my country. Like my sister's name, Emily *Michelle*."

I have such a big mouth. I should learn to shut it sometimes.

Michel did not look pleased to meet me.

"Yes. Well, *Christopher,* is this yours?" He held up the shoe he was holding, an enormous Doc Marten. Like, size 13.

Whoa. That was low. Very low.

Before I could answer, a sweet-looking girl walked up to me, carrying my sneaker. "Hi. I'm Shoshana. A girl named Mallory told me this is yours."

"'Let's Go, Mets'?" Michel said, reading my scribble. "Your taste in baseball teams matches your taste in sneakers. Blue Jays all the way!"

I snatched my sneaker and stormed away. "Show me to your group, Shoshana."

"Aren't I supposed to meet *your* group?" Michel asked.

I let out a loud whistle. A dozen or so heads turned toward me. "Guys," I announced, "this is Michel."

That was it. I had done my job. I hoped I wouldn't ever have to see that creep again.

CHAPTER 5

Claudia

Greetings from sunny, ~~appeczotic~~ Stoneybrook.   monday
Wish you were hear.
Wish I was their.
    Todays our 1st day on the job, & allready
we had a crisis. See, 2 of the counselers, this
brother and sister, didn't show up. 1 of them
was surposed to be a head counseler. And
they didn't' tell any one untill yestrday.
    So Ms. Garsia called 1 of the had
counselers to recroot somebody. That head
counseler was Jerry micheals.
    I'll' give you one geuss who he picked....

"Now, we have a lot to do before the children arrive," Ms. Garcia was saying. "But first, some news. As you notice, we have a new head counselor. . . ."

It can't be true, I thought.

"Our original head counselor, Tiffany Sweet, could not be with us. . . ." Ms. Garcia droned on.

I made a mental note never, *ever* to talk to Tiffany again.

". . . And I'm happy to say Jerry Michaels has found us a wonderful replacement. . . ."

I could have gone on that trip to Europe. But I hadn't wanted to. I had *preferred* to stay in Stoneybrook. I'd never been a counselor in a real, official camp before. And I love kids. Besides, two of my best friends — Dawn and Mary Anne — were going to be counselors. Plus Mary Anne's boyfriend, Logan. Plus Bruce Schermerhorn, who happens to be very cute. (Okay, Cokie Mason is a counselor too. She's a major pain. But hey, you can't have everything.)

My gut had told me it was the right decision.

I shouldn't always listen to my gut.

". . . So I'd like you all to welcome a young woman who gave up another summer commitment just to take her place . . ."

Smile. Pretend your life hasn't fallen apart.

". . . Janine Kishi!"

49

It was official.

My genius big sister was going to be our new co-head counselor.

I was stuck.

Everyone started clapping. *Clapping!*

Jerry, of course, was applauding the loudest. He'd called Janine the night before. She'd explained to him that she already had a job. She was supposed to be a counselor at a camp for kids with various abilities and disabilities. But that didn't stop Jerry. He said the Playground Camp would have to be canceled if she didn't join.

The liar! He had a secret motive.

LUV.

See, he and Janine used to be boyfriend and girlfriend, until Janine dumped him. Then they got back together and Janine dumped him again.

You'd think he could take a hint, but no-o-o-o.

He kept insisting. And Janine fell for it. She somehow found someone to take her place in the other camp.

Why? Beats me. Maybe she likes playing hero.

"Thanks," Janine said, blushing at the applause. "I hope I can do an adequate job. I intend to."

Adequate. That is such a Janine word.

My sister is scary smart. She'll use a three-syllable word even if a one-syllable word will do. She loves astrophysics and neurobiology. Calculus relaxes her. She's in high school, but she takes college courses.

Me? I have to work like a dog just to pass my regular classes. I was sent back a grade temporarily because of poor marks.

My parents adore Janine. The three of them share the Kishi family smart genes. (My DNA must have heard its instructions wrong. It made *art* genes by mistake.)

Don't get me wrong. I love Janine. Really.

She's just easier to take in small doses, that's all.

"We will divide the eighth-grade counselors into two groups of three," Ms. Garcia went on. "Janine will be supervising half of them: Mary Anne, Dawn . . . and, naturally, Claudia."

This was not happening.

This was *too* cruel.

Ms. Garcia rambled on and on, but I wasn't hearing a word of her speech.

Soon she was running off to talk to the SES custodian, and we were splitting into our groups.

Janine led us toward the little-kid section of the playground.

"Are you okay?" Mary Anne asked softly.

I nodded. "I'll be fine."

"Hey," Dawn whispered, "it's about the kids, remember? Everything'll change once they're here."

Mary Anne put an arm around my shoulder. "We're all together. This'll be fun."

My friends are *so* cool. They read my mind.

"Thanks," I said.

"Come along!" Janine called over her shoulder. "I suppose we should check the equipment, as a precaution."

Check the equipment? Puh-leeze.

Dawn, Mary Anne, and I pulled on the swings. We felt the seesaw for splintery wood. We checked the sandbox for broken glass. Janine reached into the mouth of the fiberglass tyrannosaurus. (Why? To check for half-eaten chunks of fiberglass triceratops, I guess.)

After awhile I had nothing else to do. So I hopped on a swing.

So did Dawn and Mary Anne. In a moment, we were pumping hard, soaring toward the treetops.

"Uh, girls . . . ?" Janine said.

Jerry was bounding over to us. "Hey, isn't anybody working here?"

"We're finished," I informed him.

"Oh. I see. Special little-sister privileges, huh?" Jerry remarked. "Lucky girl."

Janine adjusted her glasses. "I beg your pardon?" she said coldly.

"Just kidding," Jerry replied. "Don't sweat it. Everything's fine. Most of the important stuff is nearly done."

He gestured toward the other part of the playground. Bruce was using a little wheeled thing to make chalk lines on the baseball field. Logan was on a ladder, attaching new nets to the basketball hoops. (Cokie was holding the ladder and looking at her nails.)

"For your information, Jerry," Janine said, "child safety is very important."

"Hey, I was *joking*!"

"We *were* working hard," Janine pressed on. "And for your information, Claudia receives no special treatment at all."

"Okay, okay," Jerry replied. As he turned to go, he called out, "Yo, Cokie! After you're done, go find out where the first-aid stuff is!"

Janine was glaring at him. Her lips were pursed.

I knew that look. I see it whenever I borrow something from her without asking. Or when I play my music too loud while she's deep into astrophysics.

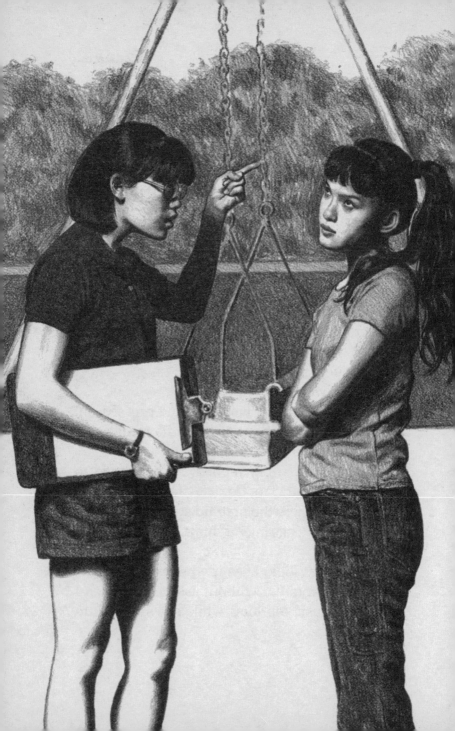

The Janine Kishi *I-must-stay-in-control* look.

"Claudia," she said, "when you're finished goofing off, would you please greet the children as they come in?"

Goofing off?

I stayed calm. I did not yell. I was not going to let her ruin my summer.

I dug my feet into the dirt beneath the swing and hopped off.

"Sure, Janine," I said sweetly.

Janine turned to Dawn. "Maybe you and Ms. Garcia can bring out a table, to facilitate signing in. And Mary Anne, some extra name tags might be wise, until we know all the children by sight. And Claudia, while you're talking to the parents, be sure they know that the children must have their immunization and health forms by today or they will not be admitted. . . ."

As I walked away, nodding, I forced myself to smile.

"I *will* have fun," I chanted under my breath. "I *will* have fun. I *will* have fun. . . ."

CHAPTER 6

Mallory

Tuesday

As the Thames ripples silently outside, through the Tate Gallery windows, like the flowing of my life

The day grows old, and I feel tortured, like the portraits by William Blake

Forget it.

I'm supposed to write VIBRANTLY. I'm supposed to USE the details around me to reflect what I feel inside. That's what Mr. D says.

But I can't do it. I can't concentrate.

56

It's 5:30. The Tate Gallery is about to close. Our group was supposed to leave half an hour ago.

The problem is, my cousin was supposed to meet me here between 4:30 and 4:45, then take me to her house for dinner.

So everyone's staying late because of me.

Another problem is, I don't know what my cousin looks like.

This exhausts me. So I'm taking a break. Sitting under a Turner painting of a dark, turbulent sea.

Which describes the state of my stomach right this moment. . . .

"Attention," a voice echoed into the gallery room. "We will be closing in ten minutes. Please proceed to the nearest exit."

The visitors in the room started heading out. I had my eye on one of them.

Glasses. Red hair. A spray of freckles across the nose. A musical laugh.

So much like the photo of Gillian Orton that Mom had shown me.

But the image was at least twelve years old. Taken before I was born, when Mom was visiting England. Gillian would look a lot different now.

I tried to age the picture in my mind.

It was a match. Or close enough.

"Gillian?" I said to the woman.

She stopped laughing. "Beg pardon?"

"Never mind."

This was ridiculous.

I had had this conversation about four times already. London is *full* of red-haired, freckle-faced women my mom's age. And they all hang out at the Tate Gallery.

Ms. McGill was peeking nervously into the room. Most of the other kids had moved on to another exhibit.

"I'm sorry, honey," she said. "But I can't find

Mr. Dougherty, and the Berger chaperones have already left with their kids, so I need to keep an eye on —"

"It's okay," I said, walking toward her. "I guess we should go."

"Madam!" someone was calling from the opposite door. "Pardon me, but the gallery is closing."

Ms. McGill turned toward the voice, nodding politely.

But the guard was yelling at someone else. An anxious-looking woman with a huge mop of salt-and-pepper hair. As she ran toward us, a man and two blond children followed her, trying to keep up.

"Pardon me," the woman called out, "you don't happen to be from the Stoneyfield School . . . ?"

"Brook," said the older boy, who looked about nine or ten.

"Gillian?" I said.

"Mallory?" she replied.

Hallelujah. I was finally right.

Cousin Gillian threw her arms around me. "I thought so! I'm so sorry. You see — oh, my dear, you are the spitting image of your mother! — I was in the middle of a particularly difficult chapter, and my agent called — you must have thought I'd forgotten about you — Bernard, Brett, this is your second cousin Mallory! And this is my husband, Peter!"

I was out of breath just listening. "Hi," I said to the two boys. They were dressed in neatly pressed school uniforms, and they politely shook my hand.

"I'm eight, but most people think I'm older," Bernard volunteered. "Brett is five, but most people think he's younger."

"Five and five-twelfths!" Brett corrected him.

"Peter Orton," Gillian's husband introduced himself. He was a tall, trim man with a blond beard, wearing a linen jacket and gabardine pants. "Welcome to London."

I shook his hand, then introduced them all to Ms. McGill, who looked very relieved. She quickly excused herself and hurried off.

Gillian put her arm around me as we walked to the exit. "I never should have agreed to this impossible deadline," she said. "Especially with a so-called full-time job that forces me to squeeze my writing into the *worst* time of the day, right after school. Sorry, darlings, it's my *favorite* time, of course, just not conducive to writing, you see —"

"Mom never told me you were a writer," I said.

"A novelist," Mr. Orton said. "And a very good one."

"An *unpublished* novelist," Gillian said with a laugh. "Although I do have a contract for a book to *be* published. Aside from my publisher, my agent, and certain privileged members of my family, no one knows that I write. It's our little secret. The university wouldn't look kindly on one of their economics professors dabbling in popular fiction."

"I'm a writer too!" exclaimed Brett, the younger son.

"In a language no one can recognize," Bernard commented.

"Mummy, he's teasing me!" Brett squealed.

"Boys, please," Gillian said. "Anyway, I now have a deadline, which is why I was working so hard today and lost track of time. So please forgive me."

Forgive her?

All that waiting in the gallery, all that anxiety — *poof*. Forgotten.

My cousin was a real, live writer.

A professor *and* a writer.

I was so impressed.

"Can I read your manuscript?" I asked.

Gillian laughed. "I wouldn't want to bore you."

"You won't! I think it's cool that you're a writer. I am too. I mean, I want to be one."

Mr. Orton smiled proudly. "It runs in the family."

"Will you read *my* book?" Brett asked. "It's smashing! It's about an owl and a kitty cat —"

"Pussycat," Bernard corrected him. "And you're just *copying*."

"Am not!"

"Are too!"

"Ahem!" said Mr. Orton.

They sounded just like my brothers.

I knew I was going to feel right at home.

The Ortons lived in a gorgeous neighborhood called Chelsea, with elegant brick townhouses on quiet, winding, tree-lined streets, not far from the River Thames.

"This feels so Dickensian!" I exclaimed, climbing out of the Ortons' BMW.

"A bit more sinister," Gillian said. "Bram Stoker lived in this neighborhood . . . the author of *Dracula*."

"Really? Can we visit his house?" I asked.

"Come see my room!" Brett was pulling on my arm.

"Go ahead," Gillian said. "It may not be Bram Stoker, but it has its own horrific elements."

So upstairs I went with my little cousins.

Each of them had his own room on the third story (or second, depending on how you counted). Gillian had been right. The messes on their floors reminded me of my own brothers' rooms.

But the rest of the story was pretty amazing — slanting eaves, creaky wood floors, and a polished wooden wardrobe in each room.

"This is so cool," I said, standing in the vestibule at the top of the stairs.

"Cool. It's really cool. Way cool. Like, like." Brett was beaming. "Do I sound American?"

Bernard groaned. "Don't you have *any* manners?"

"Want to see my cool book?" Without waiting for an answer, Brett raced into his room and returned with a sheaf of construction paper fastened into a book shape with about a hundred staples along the left side. Each page was full of scribbles and random letters that seemed to be arranged into words, some backward and some forward.

"I told you it was gibberish," Bernard remarked, pulling me by the hand toward his room. "My artwork won first prize this week," he added.

"She has to read it!" Brett shouted.

"How can she? It's written in *Brettish*!"

"Shoo! Shoo! Who let a smelly old Saint *Bernard* in the house?"

Oops. Time to shift into baby-sitter mode.

"Have you guys ever thought of collaborating?" I asked.

Blank looks.

"For example," I continued, "C. S. Lewis wrote the words to *The Lion, the Witch, and the Wardrobe*, but a different person illustrated it. Bernard, with your artwork and Brett's stories, you could make a book together."

A smile spread across Brett's face. "That is so so *so* way cool!"

Bernard looked a little more reluctant. "Well, I suppose if you let me help you write letters straight . . ."

By the time Gillian called us to dinner, I could not get the boys out of Bernard's room. Mr. Orton had to come upstairs.

"We're working!" Brett protested.

"May we eat after you do?" Bernard asked.

"Of course." Mr. Orton grinned. "Mallory, if you are ever in the market for a nanny position . . ."

And that's how I ended up eating a nice, cozy dinner alone with Gillian and Peter Orton.

We gossiped about our families. Gillian explained that my mom's family was originally

64

from Ireland and England, but one branch moved to the U.S. in the 1950s.

"Gillian has researched the family tree," Mr. Orton said. "Show it to her, Gillian. I'll feed the tigers."

Gillian led me into a gorgeous oak-paneled library, carpeted with Persian rugs. As she looked through the shelves, I sank into a crimson leather armchair that was angled to face a fireplace. I imagined myself in a cardigan, sipping tea and thinking deeply about the plot for my next highly awaited novel.

"Here it is," said Gillian. She sat in the armchair next to mine and opened a large, leatherbound book on her lap.

At the top of the page was the name BENNETT (my mom's maiden name). My glance slid down to the bottom of the page. Part of it (the important part) looked like this:

Mallory

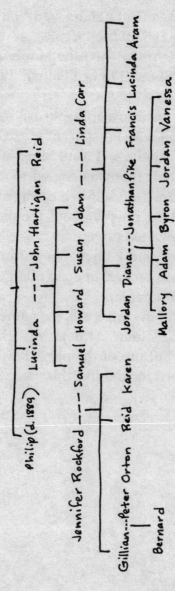

There I was.

Published.

I felt goose bumps all over.

"But it's not complete," I said. "Brett's not there, and neither are my brother Nicky and my sisters Margo and Claire."

"The book is already eight years old. It needs to be updated." Gillian had a funny smile on her face. "I think you'll find it interesting to go further back into the past, Mallory. Particularly since you want to be a writer."

I flipped the pages backward. The book was divided into chapters. Each chapter represented a span of years. It began with interesting tidbits about the family lines. The further I read, the more complicated the family lines became.

I was swept away by the flood of names. Some of the family lines branched off into question marks or were connected by vague, dotted lines. But a few of them kept going back and back . . . through the seventeen hundreds . . . the sixteen hundreds . . .

"There!" Gillian suddenly shouted as I turned to a page near the front.

At the top of the page, a name was circled.

It was no bigger than any of the others, but when I saw it, I nearly fainted:

William Shakespeare

CHAPTER 7

Stacey

Tuesday

Eureka. Mallory's cousins have arrived.

I don't Know WHAT took them so long.

I am dying at this gallery. We were supposed to be at Harrods by now, the ONE place I absolutely HAVE to go to. But no. We had to wait. On this of all days. After I've spent an entire morning and afternoon being stared at by tourists, wondering why on EARTH this otherwise normal-looking girl is dressed like a middle-aged woman.

And NOW we have another delay.

Mr. Dougherty. No one's seen him for about two hours. Mom's freaking out.
Now she's our only chaperone.
<u>I'm</u> freaking out.
WE'LL NEVER LEAVE!

"Gray hair. A handlebar mustache. Tweed jacket. He answers to Fred Dougherty." Mom was in Frantic Mode.

The security guard repeated the description into his walkie-talkie.

"I'll check the shop!" Ms. Post said, running off.

"Please hurry!" Mom called out. "Stacey is a diabetic and has to eat a meal within the hour — and if we don't make it to Harrods, she'll have no clothing to wear!"

"Really?" I heard Alan Gray's goony voice say.

Everyone else was cracking up.

Me? I was melting into the floor.

I wanted to fall asleep, wake up, and discover this was all one big, horrible nightmare.

Half the group had already split off to go to Harrods with Mr. LaVigne and the Berger chaperones. I, of course, had to stay with Mom's group and track down Mr. D.

Grrrrr.

"What if he's been mugged?" Abby asked.

"Or kidnapped," Jessi added.

"Maybe Louis Anderson has him," Kristy suggested. "As we speak, he's writing a ransom note: 'I will return Mr. Dougherty if you return my ashes, no questions asked.'"

"Not funny," I grumbled.

To add insult to injury, Jacqui Grant was still slobbering all over Robert. She had him practically pinned against the wall. They were comparing prints they'd bought at the shop.

"You actually like that?" she asked, grimacing at one of Robert's choices. "It looks like something my five-year-old brother could paint."

Robert shrugged. "I thought it looked cool."

"*This* one looks cool," Jacqui said, unrolling one of her prints. "The guy in it? He's supposed to be a god or something? He looks just like you!"

Robert rolled his eyes, red-faced. He glanced at me as if to say, "Help!"

I wanted to vomit.

Mom was pacing the floor now. "Are you all right, Stacey?" she asked me.

"Yes, Mom," I said.

"Not too tired or hungry?"

"No, Mom."

"*I'm* hungwy," whined Alan Gray in a mock baby voice. "*When are we gonna eat?*"

His voice resounded in the Tate Gallery's front lobby. People turned to look.

"We've never seen that guy before," announced Kristy. "He's not with our group."

Kristy's pick-a-shoe partner was by her side. Michel Something. That seemed weird. She had

71

told me she detested him. She said he was a Canadian Alan Gray. (He sure was cuter than Alan. Even in my sour state I could tell that.)

Michel was snickering. "Don't any of you have manners in public?"

"No way," Alan said proudly. "In America, we like to speak our minds."

"If that were true, you'd be silent," Abby murmured.

Michel glowered at Alan. "In *America*? As opposed to where?"

"*Your* country," Alan replied, rolling his eyes. "It's called Canada. *Duh*."

"Alaaaan," I warned.

"Hey, that's funny. Cana*duh*!" Alan said.

"For your information, Canada is part of America too," Michel said, stepping toward Alan. "You live in a country called the United States."

"Uh, guys? If you want to pick a fight, do it outside," Kristy said.

"Yeah!" Alan agreed. "Kristy will beat you up!"

Michel laughed. "Is she your girlfriend?"

"*NO WAY!*" Kristy blurted out.

"She wishes," Alan murmured.

I thought Kristy was going to slug both of them.

Instead she stormed away.

For a moment — just a moment — I felt a little better. At least I wasn't the only miserable person around.

"Ohhhhh, what a rogue and peasant slave am I!" a deep voice echoed in the room.

We all spun around. Mr. Dougherty was strolling toward us, followed by a harried-looking Ms. Post.

Mr. D's mustache curled upward with his broad smile. He was loaded down with shopping bags. "So sorry," he continued. "I slipped away to see the pre-Raphaelites for a moment, and I spotted a painting I *had* to own, so I scurried to the Gallery Shop — quick, quick — to buy a print, but I was sidetracked by the Whistler mural in the restaurant, and . . ."

I was the first one out the door. I didn't even wait to hear him finish. I could not believe how immature he was being.

Mom followed right behind me. She had murder in her eyes. I could hear her muttering something about "inappropriate behavior."

Ms. Post led us to the nearest station of the Underground, or tube (which is what Londoners call their subway).

We piled into the first arriving car. Robert sat on one of the few empty seats, looked at me, and gestured toward the place next to him.

"The *tube!*" Jacqui squealed as she plopped

down into the seat. "That's the nickname for the subway. That is *so* cool!"

Not. My. Problem, I told myself.

We rode two stops on the Victoria Line to the Green Park station, then switched to the Piccadilly Line and rode two more stops to the Knightsbridge station. (Got that? If you've grown up using the NYC subways, navigating London is no sweat, although it's hard to adjust to the cleanliness.)

How was Harrods? Well, let's put it this way. It was like stepping into Bloomingdale's, Macy's, Zabar's, and half of Fifth Avenue all rolled into one. (If you don't recognize those names, you *must* visit New York.)

Forget Buckingham Palace. Forget Paris.

I was in heaven.

The moment I stepped into the store, I zoomed off to the designer dresses.

"Bulletin. We have finally located the real Stacey," Abby said. "Send fireworks."

My shop-stravaganza was interrupted only once, for high tea (which is what the British call an early dinner) at a restaurant right in Harrods. There we met the other group, and then we *all* shopped.

I must have picked out twenty fabulous outfits.

Mom must have had twenty heart attacks when she looked at the price tags.

We ended up buying two of the outfits — one for the theater that night and one for daytime sightseeing. "To tide you over until your suitcase is returned," Mom said.

Arguing did no good. (Sigh.) I took what I could get.

All of my friends found wonderful things — well, all except Kristy. She bought a pack of white crew socks. Also, she spent the whole shopping trip arguing with Michel. Something about baseball. I couldn't understand it.

As we took the tube back to the hotel, I was feeling so-o-o-o much better. I wasn't mad at Mom. I wasn't thinking about those ashes. I didn't care that Jacqui was showing off her new clothes to Robert. Or that Robert kept looking at me, as if he wanted me to rescue him. Or that Kristy and Michel were still at it. Or that Abby had started a singalong of Elvis songs, right in the train.

I was so psyched about going to the theater in my new dress that I flew into my hotel room without even noticing that the telephone message light was blinking.

Mom had followed me in, to drop off one of my bags. When she saw the light, she quickly picked up the receiver. "Hello? . . . Yes? . . . He did? Where is he?" She took a pen out of the nightstand and scribbled on a notepad:

L. ANDERSON
HÔTEL DES GRANDES ÉCOLES
RUE DU CARDINAL-LEMOINE
43.26.79.23

As she was writing, Kristy came in and glanced over her shoulder. "That's the guy!" she mouthed to me.

Mom said good-bye, hung up, and tapped out the phone number she'd written. "He's in Paris, not London," she said over her shoulder. "Apparently he called the airline around the same time we did, and he has your suitcase."

"Yyyyyes!" Kristy shouted.

"You're not going to make me return the new clothes, are you?" I asked.

Mom ignored me. "Hello?" she said into the receiver. "Is this Mr. Anderson? Hi, I'm Maureen McGill. I believe my daughter and you switched luggage . . . yes, I know . . . Oh? Oh, dear . . ." Mom's face fell.

Kristy and I gave each other a Look.

My stomach growled.

Mom muttered a few "Mm-hm's" and "Oh, my's" before saying good-bye. When she hung up, she looked pretty grim. "Well, the good news is that Mr. Anderson is a very nice man, and he's offered to make arrangements with the airline to deliver your suitcase here tomorrow."

"And the bad news?" Kristy asked.

"Well, it seems Mr. Anderson is a World War Two veteran," Mom replied. "The ashes in his suitcase belong to his platoon buddy, Dennis. They stormed the beach together at Normandy, France, on D-Day."

"He's been carrying around the ashes since then?" Kristy asked.

"No," Mom said softly. "Dennis died this year. On his deathbed, he asked Mr. Anderson to scatter his ashes at Normandy. So that's why he's in France."

"So we'll send him his suitcase, and everything'll be fine," I said.

Mom shook her head. "I didn't feel right about trusting the ashes to the airline, Stacey. Neither did he. So he asked if *we'd* deliver them when we arrive in Paris."

"Of course you told him no," I said.

"How could I?" Mom sighed. "I'm afraid I agreed."

I slumped onto the bed.

Playing messenger with a cremated body. What a way to spend a vacation.

* * *

I thought about those ashes all evening.

Why would a grown man ask someone to scatter his remains on a beach halfway around the world? Wouldn't he want his ashes to be near his friends and family? And why would another man actually travel all the way to Europe to do this for him? I mean, okay, they were in the war together. That was important. But it was over fifty years ago.

It seemed weird. Morbid.

I thought about it even during the theater. It didn't help that the play was a revival of the musical *Shenandoah*, which was about war and death. (The Civil War, though, not World War II.)

That night I had trouble getting to sleep.

I was deep in the the middle of a dream when Mom woke me the next morning.

She was grinning. "Wake up, you two. Time for our morning trip."

"Rrraumpf?" Kristy grumbled sleepily.

"To where?" I asked.

"The Cabinet War Rooms," Mom explained. "Where Winston Churchill and his cabinet hid underground during World War Two, planning the strategy that won the war."

Ugh. My beauty sleep was being ruined for the sake of a *war exhibit*?

"Must we?" I asked.

"Just think of how knowledgeable you'll be if Mr. Anderson starts talking about the war."

Kristy was hopping out of bed already. "Cool."

"Meet you in the lobby," Mom said.

I was outnumbered.

It was a good thing Mom had asked the hotel staff to launder the outfit I had worn on the airplane. I dragged myself out of bed and threw it on.

Minutes later we were wolfing down croissants and orange juice with our group at the breakfast buffet. Then we dashed outside to the tube and rode it to Westminster station.

Once we arrived at the Cabinet War Rooms exhibit, we stepped down into a corridor of dark, windowless rooms.

The rooms were two stories underground. They were also covered by solid concrete ten feet thick.

"Bombproof," Mom remarked. "In the U.S., people didn't experience stuff like this. But the Nazis conducted air raids on London for years."

You know what popped into my mind? *The Lion, the Witch, and the Wardrobe*. I had never really understood why Peter, Susan, Edmund, and Lucy were sent away from their London home during the war. "Air raids," was what the book said, but that never meant anything to me.

Now it did. The kids were sent away so they wouldn't be blown to bits.

And during all this, the British military leaders were in this cramped, tiny hole.

Living deep underground.

We looked into the rooms, through Plexiglas barriers. Papers were piled on the desks and maps still hung on the walls, covered with little flag markers. As if the war leaders had just stepped out for tea and were about to return.

I could hear snatches of what our tour guide was saying.

"The bombing went on for years, and the mood down here was awful, until a bleak morning in June of 1944, when one of the boldest strategies was set in motion. Thousands of American, British, and Canadian troops launched an all-out surprise attack. It was called Operation Overlord, and it began on a lonely beach in Normandy, France. After this landing, the tide of the war changed. The Allies pushed across Europe and never looked back. . . ."

And Mr. Anderson had been there. Making the world safe again. Changing history. With his friend Dennis. Maybe eighteen, nineteen years old.

All because of a plan that was developed here.

"It's so cool that they left all this stuff," Kristy whispered.

It *was* cool. But what about guys like Mr. Anderson and Mr. Petropoulos? What did they have to leave? They weren't protected by a bombproof cave. How could anyone know about what *they* did?

A chill ran through me.

And I thought about those ashes again.

This time I didn't think they were weird at all.

I was glad Mom hadn't let the airline take them.

I wanted to give them to Mr. Anderson myself.

CHAPTER 8

Mary Anne

Wednesday
Day Three of Playground
Camp.
Three days of laughs
and fun times and HARD
WORK.
Two and a half days
of good weather.
The bad half happened
today. ☹ It's a good thing
we were prepared.
Well, some of us were....

"Everybody inside!" shouted Ms. Garcia.

"But it's not raining!" whined Marilyn Arnold.

KA-BOOOOOM! cracked a sudden blast of thunder.

"TORNADO!" shouted Melody Korman.

"Waaaaaah!" screamed Suzi Barrett.

The weather had been fine. A bit muggy and overcast, pretty typical for a Stoneybrook summer afternoon. No rain had been predicted.

So the sudden dark clouds took us completely by surprise.

I lifted Suzi out of the sandbox. Her brother, Buddy, was playing a game of basketball with Linny Papadakis. "Come on, guys," I said.

"But we're in a best-of-five playoff!" Linny protested.

"You can use the gym inside," I said.

"Yyyyes! You *die*, Buddy!" shouted Linny, running toward the school door.

Out of the corner of my eye, I saw Claudia gathering up a big, messy papier-mâché project with Carolyn Arnold, Jake Kuhn, and Lindsey DeWitt.

Janine was standing over them, hands on hips. Yelling at Claudia. Telling her that papier-mâché was not an "appropriate outdoor project."

I wish Janine wouldn't be so hard on Claudia.

83

MaryAnne

The rain started falling as we ran to the door. Not gradually, either. It seemed as if the clouds had ruptured, like water balloons.

I deposited the kids and dashed outside again to help Claudia and Janine. We managed to rescue the papier-mâché before it could cement the whole playground.

Claudia and I were giggling as we stepped inside. Our clothes were soaked through and through.

"Do we have everyone?" Janine called out.

"Yes, General Janine," Cokie Mason said.

"One, two, three . . ." Janine ran off, counting heads.

The gym was just down the hall. I could hear thudding basketballs and squeals of joy from within.

"Girls, will you be in charge of setting up the video apparatus?" Ms. Garcia called out to us. "The AV office is open."

"Sure!" Claudia replied.

We were dripping as we walked down the hall.

Cokie Mason was sinking to the hallway floor, next to the soda machine. As we passed, she started cracking up. "Well, if it isn't the Baby-sitters Club wet T-shirt contest. Not that anyone would notice."

"Stuff it, Cokie," Claudia said.

"I don't have to," Cokie replied.

"Between the ears you do," said Claudia.

I hate insults. I think they are so depressing and destructive. But I have to admit, I wish I could have thought of that.

Cokie had not been an ideal counselor so far. In fact, she'd been more like a camper. We'd been cleaning up after her messes. We'd had to call her in for lunch. And she hardly ever seemed to want to play with the kids.

"It just isn't right," I said under my breath as we walked into the AV room. "She doesn't do her fair share. She doesn't even seem to want to *be* here."

"Her parents forced her," Claudia said.

"But she still had to pass the tryout, like the rest of us. She must have shown some enthusiasm and dedication."

"You don't understand, Mary Anne. Her mom is on the Board of Ed. The Board of Ed runs this camp. It's, like, this political thing."

"But that's horrible!"

Claudia shrugged. "That's life."

As we loaded the equipment onto a cart, Janine came flying into the room. "Where's Mathew Hobart?"

"How should I know?" Claudia retorted.

"He's missing," Janine shot back. "I counted only forty-nine kids in there."

"Are you sure?" asked Cokie, walking up behind her.

Janine spun around. "I can count."

"Well, you're not *perfect*!" Cokie said.

Janine ran back into the hallway. Claudia and I dropped what we were doing and followed her.

Jerry was barreling toward us. "Did you find him?"

"No!" Janine replied, heading for the door. "Whose group was he in?"

"Cokie's," Jerry replied.

I shot Cokie a Look.

"Is that the Australian kid?" she asked.

"Yes!" Jerry said.

Cokie shrugged. "I *told* him to come in."

I didn't wait to hear Jerry's response. I was out the door in a flash.

The rain hit me in the face, making me squint.

Claudia was running toward the baseball field. Janine was heading for the climbing equipment.

I swerved to the left, into the little-kid area.

Nothing.

As I turned to leave, I saw the flash of red.

It was behind a thick maple tree.

Mary Anne

I spun back and ran toward it.

In the rain, Mathew's red hair looked even brighter. The rest of his body was brown, from the huge mud pile he was playing in.

"*What are you doing out here?*" I shouted.

Mathew looked startled. "Playing!" he replied.

I took his arm, but it slipped out of my grip. "You can't stay out here in a thunderstorm, under a tree!"

"Why?" he asked.

KA-BOOOOOM!

The flash of lightning bathed the entire playground in a momentary greenish light.

Mathew grinned. "Cool."

I grabbed him under his armpits and lifted him off his feet. "We are going in right now."

"Stop! You're not my counselor! Cokie is!"

He tried to slip out of my grasp. I held tight.

I could see Janine and Claudia now, racing toward me.

"Help me!" I shouted.

"*Stop!*" Mathew yelled.

Cokie was going to pay for this.

I didn't know how, but she was.

CHAPTER 9

Jessi

Wednesday
Announcing ... today's
European Jessi Awards!

Weirdest Impromptu Trip:
Madame Tussaud's
Waxworks. We went
in the morning, while
Ms. McGill took
another group to a
bomb shelter or
something. I talked
to the President, and
I showed Michael
Jackson some dance
moves.

Jessi

Grossest Exhibit:
The body of the
"Celtic Lindow Man"
at the British Museum —
a human sacrifice
whose body was
preserved for
centuries in a bog
(yuck).

Creepiest Place:
The Tower of London,
where prisoners were
locked up before
being beheaded. You
can still read the
desperate messages
they scratched into
the stones!

Most Embarrassing
Moment:
Kristy howling like
a dog in public,
just because Michel
was playing this
harmonica he'd bought.

Scariest Moment:
Losing Mr. Dougherty
in the Smithfield
Market.

Best Moment...
(drum roll, please):
Toni Lobel, Mr.
Brailsford's assistant,
returning the call
I left for her at
the Barbican Centre
yesterday — And
Saying She Reserved
Six Tickets For
Tonight's Dance
NY Performance!

Jessi

My stomach was in knots. As we walked away from the River Thames and across the Victoria Embankment Gardens, I could see the Barbican Centre. It was a humongous building.

Around me, my friends were chattering away. I couldn't believe how relaxed they were.

"He is such a jerk," Kristy grumbled. "I mean, playing a harmonica on a public sidewalk?"

"Uh, Kristy?" Abby said. "Can we switch the topic? You've been talking about Michel since lunch."

Stacey raised her eyes from a book about World War II she was reading. "You must really hate him a lot, huh, Kristy?"

Kristy glared at her. "What's that supposed to mean?"

"Oh, nothing," Stacey said sweetly.

"You know, you shouldn't read and walk at the same time," Abby said. "You can get vertigo. Or maybe it's gout."

"No, really, Stacey," Kristy insisted. "Are you trying to *imply* something? Are you suggesting I might actually have the slightest non-negative feeling for that —"

"Oh, look, is that the place?" Stacey asked.

"Must be," Ms. McGill replied.

People were flocking toward the entrance.

Talking, laughing. Looking forward to a night of fabulous dancing.

I wanted to be just like them. I should have been. This was the part of the vacation I'd looked forward to the most.

But my mind was sabotaging me. All I could think about was where I *could* have been.

I pictured myself backstage. Doing *barre* stretches. Adjusting my makeup. Feeling the energy of the audience through the curtains. The houselights dimming . . .

Stop.

I could not do this to myself.

I closed my eyes for a moment. I took a deep breath.

I was going to enjoy this if it killed me.

"So this thing is just *ballet*?" Kristy asked.

Abby rolled her eyes. "I hear there's a slam-dunk competition after the first act."

"It's more than ballet," I explained. "The choreography uses lots of different music and dance styles — jazz, Brazilian, Afro-Cuban. . . ."

Mallory nodded. "I'm no dancer, and I loved Jessi's concert in Stamford."

"Guess I should learn to like this stuff," Kristy said with a sigh. "Someday you could be in this company, Jessi. Then I'll *have* to come see it."

Kristy didn't know how close she was to the truth.

Jessi

Besides my family, no one knows that Mr. Brailsford had offered me a spot in the permanent company. And that I'd said no.

I hadn't wanted to spread the news. I hadn't wanted my friends to second-guess me. To tell me I was crazy.

Besides, Mr. Brailsford had assured me the spot would be open if I ever wanted to return. I planned to take him up on it someday.

If he would even remember me.

I took deep, slow breaths as we walked into the Barbican.

The place was overwhelming. Like a city in itself. The directory inside listed two theaters, a concert hall, an art gallery, a cineplex, and lots of shops and cafés.

Abby let out a whistle. "A little bit of Washington Mall, right here in London!"

"Such a philistine," Mallory said in mock disgust.

We looked at her blankly.

"That means *a person without culture*," she said. "Mr. Dougherty taught it to us."

I could see Ms. McGill's face tighten. Mr. Dougherty was not her favorite topic of conversation these days. Earlier I had overheard her calling him "Frederick the Wanderer" to Ms. Post. Even the Berger chaperones were complaining about him.

Jessi

In the distance I could see a Dance NY banner hanging from a rafter.

My heart started to race.

We found the box office, picked up our tickets (fifteenth row center), and walked into the concert hall.

The place was practically empty. We were way early.

"Jessi?" a voice rang out from behind me.

I turned. *"Tanisha!"*

I screamed. She screamed. We flew into each other's arms and then screamed some more.

I quickly introduced everyone. Tanisha said hi, then checked her watch. "It's almost time for half-hour call. Jessi, you *have* to come backstage and say hi!"

I looked at Ms. McGill.

"Just be back here in time for the show," she said.

"Thanks!" I was off like a shot.

I followed Tanisha through a curtain on the side of the house. We wound through some corridors and then downstairs to a green room in the basement. (It wasn't really green. That's just the traditional name for a big backstage gathering place for performers.)

Toni was the first to see me. She swept me up in a big hug.

Some of Tanisha's friends remembered me. *I,*

Jessi

of course, knew everyone in the company. They were some of the best dancers in the world.

As I was chattering with them, Mr. Brailsford walked into the room.

I knew he was there even before I saw him. His presence is so big, it electrifies the air.

"Well, if it isn't my prima ballerina Jessica Ramsey!"

He remembered me!

How did I stay upright? I don't know. It wasn't easy. My knees almost gave out.

"Hi," I squeaked.

"What a pleasure!" (I love — *love* — his West Indies accent.) "Are you seeing the show?"

"Yup."

"Good. Come back again afterward and give us notes." He grinned and backed out the door. "We sure do miss you, Jessica."

As he disappeared down the corridor, I nearly leaped through the ceiling.

I have no idea what we talked about after that. I was in a daze.

All I remember is Tanisha leading me out the door when it was time to go.

I didn't snap back to reality until I heard a scream.

It was loud. Painful.

We ran to the source of it, a practice room at the end of the hall.

Mr. Brailsford was in there. So was a woman who must have been a doctor or nurse. They were both leaning over a dancer who was sprawled out on the floor. I recognized her. Clarissa Jones, one of the younger corps members.

The rest of the company was now running out of the green room and into the hallway behind Tanisha and me.

Mr. Brailsford stood up slowly, leaving the woman to tend to Clarissa. He came into the corridor, closing the door behind him.

The star power was gone from his face. He looked as if he'd aged.

"What happened?" Tanisha asked.

"Clarissa sprained her ankle warming up," he said. "She won't be able to go on tonight."

"Where's Yolanda?" someone asked.

"In her hotel room." Mr. Brailsford heaved a sigh. "Food poisoning."

I gave Tanisha a curious glance.

"The understudy," she whispered.

I could see the wheels turning in Mr. Brailsford's head. "Okay, we'll be able to handle *Brasilica* with some minor changes," he said. "And Clarissa's not in *Striver's Row.* . . ."

He ran through the schedule, number by number, making revisions. Toward the end he paused. He thought for a moment, then shook

Jessi

his head. "The problem is *Gotham Rhythm*. Without Clarissa, the symmetry is shot. We'll have to cancel that one, I guess."

Gotham Rhythm?

Mr. Brailsford looked up. He squinted in my direction. "Unless . . ."

No. He wouldn't.

Now he was smiling. "Jessica?"

I tried to say "What?" No sound came out.

"You know that number, don't you?" he asked. "I taught it to you."

I didn't do a thing. My head nodded itself.

He COULDN'T!

Mr. Brailsford took my hand. He pulled me down the hallway into a small room, where a harried-looking man was repairing a ballet shoe.

"Michael," Mr. Brailsford said, "I need a 'Gotham' costume for this young woman three minutes ago!"

"But — but —" I sputtered.

"Unless, of course, you're not up to it, Jessica," Mr. Brailsford said. "Which I would understand, of course. So, what'll it be?"

"Yes!" I blurted out. "I mean —"

Yes?

Had I said that?

I hadn't meant to. It was just the first word out of my mouth. But Mr. Brailsford was already running down the hall. "See me in Practice Room B for rehearsal!" he shouted.

Tanisha rushed off too. "I'll go tell your friends in the audience!" she called over her shoulder.

"Wait —"

Too late.

I was numb.

I felt as if I were floating outside myself. In a dream.

I could see smiling faces. Thumbs-up signs.

I was vaguely aware of being turned around. Of a tape measure being wrapped around various parts of me.

Before I knew it, I was being rushed into the practice room. I was stretching at the *barre*.

Mr. Brailsford arrived. He put a tape into a boom box, and I was dancing to the music of *Gotham Rhythm*.

Entrechat, chassé left, chassé right, pas de bourrée, tour jeté . . .

The steps were coming back to me. "Body memory," Mr. Brailsford called it. Even if your brain shorts out, your body remembers what it's supposed to do.

"That's it, Jessica," Mr. Brailsford said. "But on the *beat*, on the *beat* . . ."

I was rusty. I hadn't even *pliéd* for nearly a week.

Jessi

Snap. I was suddenly out of the dream.

This was insane.

"Mr. Brailsford, I changed my mind. I can't. Not on such short —"

"Costume's ready!" shouted Michael, poking his head into the room.

"I have full faith in you, Jessica," Mr. Brailsford said.

Zoom. Into the changing room. Costume on.

Soon — too soon — muffled applause filtered into the room. Followed by the music of the number before mine.

"Dancers onstage!" Mr. Brailsford called out.

Oh. My. Lord.

Go.

As I walked upstairs, Mr. Brailsford put his hand on my shoulder. Tanisha was with me, her hand holding mine.

"Tanisha, what am I doing?" I said.

"Shhhhh," she replied gently.

We emerged onto the stage. It was dark. We lined up behind the curtain.

A shudder of *déjà vu* shot through me. I wasn't sure from where. A thought, maybe. A fantasy.

I blocked it out.

"Cue orchestra," the stage manager's voice called out.

The music was starting.

Jessi

Fifteenth row center. That's where Kristy and the others were.

"Curtainnnnn . . . up!"

I was frozen. My breathing was unnatural. Too quick.

What was the first step? *I couldn't remember!*

"Tanisha, I can't . . ."

The stage light was pouring in.

"Annnnd . . . go!"

Body memory.

My legs sprang forward. As if the dance were part of me. As if I'd done it a million times.

But this was different than I remembered. *Higher.* Taller dancers. Bigger lifts from stronger arms.

I landed too hard. I slipped on a pirouette.

But I kept going. Position to position. Beat to beat.

And when I finally stopped, my heart felt as if it had ripped itself wide open. I was gasping.

It was over.

Not perfect. But I'd done it.

The dancers were scurrying into a line behind me.

"Curtain call," whispered Tanisha, grabbing my hand. "Just copy me."

We waited upstage until the principals had bowed. When Tanisha ran forward with the rest of the corps, I joined them. We all stopped and curtsied.

"YYYYYYYYESSS!   OOOH-OOOH-OOOH-OOOH!"

Even above the applause, I could hear Kristy.

I squinted. I couldn't see her or my other friends.

But I could feel them.

As the curtain came down, we had to run downstairs to make way for the next number.

Tanisha and I burst into the green room, *shrieking*.

The rest of the company (the ones who weren't in the next number) crowded around me, hugging me, congratulating me.

Mr. Brailsford was already there.

"Was I okay?" I asked.

He lifted me up. "Jessica, I am so proud of you!"

As he spun me around, the other dancers gathered in a circle and applauded.

I was crying.

But you know what? He was too.

That, I think, was the best part of the whole evening.

CHAPTER 10

Abby

Thursday

Jessi is a dancing monster! A star. Bigger than Elvis.

How did she remember all those moves? I can't even pronounce them.

Totally, totally awesome. You guys missed the performance of a lifetime.

Not to mention an unbelievable celebration afterward,

paid for by the one and only David Brailsford.

Don't feel too bad, though. The performance was taped for the BBC. We'll try to get a cassette.

I wish I had a camcorder right now. We're about to leave for yet another spectacular part of our trip — Victoria Kent's castle!

Details at eleven! Ta-ta...

Abby

Boy, had I jumped the gun.

The moment I finished writing that entry, I ran downstairs to the hotel lobby and found that our trip was doomed.

"I'm sorry, but we're just going to have to call it off," said Ms. McGill.

"We *can't*!" Stacey protested.

"The limo's on its way," Kristy reminded her.

"I know that, but I simply can't go," Ms. McGill said. "Mr. Dougherty insists on leading a literary walk, and he won't change his mind. The Berger kids are off cathedral hopping with their chaperones. *Someone* has to take the group to Hyde Park. It's on our schedule."

I felt like crying.

I'd been looking forward to this. Until a couple of weeks ago, the Kents had been living in Stoneybrook, on assignment from the British government. Their eight-year-old daughter, Victoria, was a BSC baby-sitting charge. (Actually, Mary Anne and I were the ones who spent the most time with her and knew her the best.)

Victoria is a real, live princess. If everyone in the royal family dies, and their cousins die, and then a few dozen of their cousins, *she* will be the Queen.

Or something like that. Anyway, she is technically a royal. She had told us all about her castle, complete with a moat and servants and hunting grounds.

Could I miss this? Ix-nay.

Besides, Stacey, Kristy, Jessi, Mal, and I were in our nicest clothes.

"We can go by ourselves," I suggested.

"Absolutely not," Ms. McGill snapped. "You are in a foreign country, with total strangers —"

"Mom, Sir Charles and Lady Kent are *not* strangers," Stacey insisted. "They were our neighbors."

"They might be insulted if we don't accept their invitation," Jessi added.

"We wouldn't want to cause an international incident," Kristy said solemnly.

Ms. McGill's eyes were focused on a faded Mercedes sedan that was pulling up to the curb.

The driver peered out at us. "Abigail and friends?" he said.

Well, it wasn't a coach and four horsemen, but so what? When you're invited to a castle, you can't be picky about the wheels.

Ms. McGill swallowed. We were all staring at her. "Uh, may I see your ID?" she asked the driver.

I thought Stacey was going to faint with embarrassment.

But the guy was cheerful. He pulled out a photo and a set of instructions on official government stationery with Sir Charles's name printed at the top.

"Don't worry, madam, they'll be in good hands," the driver said with a chuckle. "There will be more adults than children in the house."

A *house,* he called it. He was being cute.

The Kents were so modest.

Ms. McGill let out a big sigh. "All right. But I want you to call me when you get there and leave a message at the hotel."

"Yeeeeaaaa!" I threw my arms around Ms. McGill.

Then I jumped into the car before she could change her mind.

Kristy and Stacey joined me in the backseat, while Jessi and Mal rode up front. As the driver took off, I gave the royal wave — palm cupped, wrist pivoting ever so slightly — just like the Queen. (Ms. McGill didn't even notice.)

Kristy opened a map across her lap. "Where are we going?" she asked the driver. "Windsor Castle?"

"No," the driver said. "One of the lesser edifices."

"What?" I said.

"It means *building,*" Stacey whispered.

Okay. Fine.

The English countryside sped by. We passed through some suburban areas with low, attached houses. But before long we reached a hilly neighborhood of deep, manicured lawns and stately old trees.

As we approached a walled garden that overlooked an endless meadow, the driver slowed down.

My pulse was pounding. What a front yard! "Awesome," I said.

The driver nodded. "Best park in England, some say. It's called Hampstead Heath."

He made a turn and drove half a block. Then he pulled into the driveway of a large, Tudorstyle house with a nicely kept lawn.

Servants' quarters. Obviously.

"Here we are!" the driver exclaimed.

"Where's the castle?" Kristy asked.

The driver opened our door. As we climbed out, the front door of the house flew open, and out bustled Victoria's nanny, Miss Rutherford.

"You're here," she said. "Splendid. The roast should be ready within the hour, and —"

"Hello-o-o-o-o-o-o!"

Victoria bolted out of the house. She ran into my arms, and I swung her around.

"The Vickster!" Kristy shouted.

Victoria scrambled out of my clutches and hugged Kristy, Stacey, Jessi, and Mal. "Oh, I'm *so* happy you're all here!" she exclaimed. "Mummy was worried you'd be late, and we've so much to do to prepare for tomorrow, and it feels like *years* since I've been in the States, and don't you know that *everyone* here thinks I've gone Yank on them because of the way I speak now, and oh, this is just so . . . cool! Come!"

She took my hand and led us toward the house.

Sir Charles had appeared at the door. He was wearing a cardigan and smoking a pipe. "Well, well! So nice to see you here in our native habitat!"

"Come in, come in!" Lady Kent's voice called from inside. "You must be starved."

The place was beautiful. Ornately carved wood walls, antique furniture, hanging tapestries.

It just wasn't what I expected.

"Nice house, Vic," I said.

"Isn't it *lovely*?" she replied. "I call it Kent Castle — you know, like Windsor Castle?"

I smiled. I did not look disappointed.

I was a perfect guest.

But my heart was dragging on the Oriental rug.

We sat down for lunch in the Kents' yard, under a canopy of flowering vines. The grounds stretched before us like a golf course, ending in a small forest. Not far from the house was a tiny guest cottage with gingerbread moldings. The sight of it cheered me up.

Victoria did not stop chattering. "Mrs. Bundy, our cook, makes the most delicious sandwiches! I adore outdoor eating! You know, tomorrow I am going to meet with the Queen!"

Mm-hm, I thought. *Right here in the castle.*

Mallory's eyes were as round as baseballs. "Really?"

Sir Charles nodded. "A rather large gala at Buckingham Palace. Victoria will be presenting flowers to Her Majesty for the first time, and we are all very excited."

"Would you stand with me, Abby?" Victoria blurted out.

Huh?

"Stand?" I said. "Like, before the Queen? *The* Queen?"

"I must have a guardian," Victoria went on, "and Mummy and Daddy will be involved in the organization, and Miss Rutherford simply can't stand on her rotten ankles for more than two minutes without complaining —"

"Victoriaaaa," Lady Kent said warningly.

"I heard that!" Miss Rutherford called from inside.

"I'm only repeating what she told me!" Victoria insisted.

"Do it, Abby," Kristy urged me.

"You have to!" Stacey agreed.

Jessi and Mal were both nodding like crazy.

Abby

"If you wouldn't mind, that is," Sir Charles said. "Subject to your schedule, and your chaperones' permission, of course."

Of course. I'd have to ask. I couldn't just jump in.

"YES!" flew out of my mouth.

Me, Abigail Stevenson, meeting the Queen?

Who needs Elvis?

ROBERT

THURSDAY

HEY, GUYS. ROBERT HERE.

ENGLAND'S WAY COOL. YOU SHOULD DEFINITELY COME HERE SOMETIME. STACEY AND THE OTHERS WILL TELL YOU WHAT TO VISIT. OR MAYBE THEY HAVE ALREADY.

WELL, THAT'S ABOUT IT. SEE YOU.

ROBERT

I felt so stupid writing in the BSC journal. I told Stacey I had nothing to say. But she insisted.

Then, when she read what I wrote, she acted all disappointed.

I don't understand her.

Maybe it's just girls in general I don't understand.

Jacqui Grant especially.

She was hovering around me at the continental breakfast today. All I wanted to do was eat some pastries, hang with Pete Black, maybe read the paper.

But she sat down right next to me.

"Stacey left?" she asked.

"Uh-huh," I replied.

"For the day, right? Like to go to some castle?"

"Uh-huh."

"Is that all you can say? 'Uh-huh'?"

What was I supposed to do? I had a mouthful of Irish soda bread.

Pete was approaching. But he took one look at us, grinned, and sat at another table.

I swallowed. "Yup. To visit this princess. The one who lived in Stoneybrook for awhile."

"Cool," Jacqui said, spreading jam on her toast. "Want to go outside and smoke?"

"You *smoke*?" I said.

"Sometimes."

"I don't."

"You are too *good*, Robert." She elbowed me in the ribs and giggled.

I was not in the mood for this.

Why couldn't she leave me alone? The whole point of this trip was to get away. To have some space. Enjoy myself.

Boy, did I need that.

Before this vacation, I had been a mess.

Some days I thought life was not worth it. I had a hard time sleeping. I couldn't make the smallest decisions. Not only that, but my grades were slipping. I didn't even want to play baseball. (For me, that is *way* serious.)

Plus, I was leaning on Stacey too much. Asking her advice on everything. Treating her as if she were still my girlfriend. (She *was*, once upon a time. But we broke up.)

Stacey finally let me have it. She said I wasn't being myself.

Well, to make a long story short, I had this long talk with my baseball coach. And I started reading about depression. I learned that it can be serious. You shouldn't ignore it.

Talking about it can help.

So can a long trip.

I noticed the difference as soon as the plane lifted off. I felt like a tight knot slowly unraveling.

I sure didn't need any *new* problems. Which is why I did not want Jacqui bugging me.

I mean, Jacqui's great-looking. And she seems nice enough sometimes. But boy, does she come on strong. She hadn't left me alone since the trip began.

"So, are you going with Mr. D's group, or Ms. McGill's?" Jacqui asked. "Or one of the Berger chaperones?"

"Don't know," I replied. "You?"

"It depends."

"On what?"

Jacqui smiled. "Oh . . . on who's in which group, I guess."

Please.

I wolfed down the rest of my breakfast and stood up. "Well, guess I better get ready."

"Me too!"

Jacqui followed me to the cafeteria trash area, where I dumped my tray. Then she followed me into the lobby.

And into the lift. (It's a good thing I didn't go into the men's room. Talk about *persistent*.)

"Can I ask you something?" she said as the door slid shut.

"Sure," I replied.

"What's with you and Stacey?"

"Nothing. I mean, we're friends."

"Uh-huh. So, like, you're free. I mean, I'm just asking."

I sighed. "Yeah. I mean, if you *must* know." I did not like where this conversation seemed to be heading.

"Cool." Jacqui was grinning now. "We don't have to tell her, you know."

"Tell her *what*?"

Jacqui giggled. "You know. About *us*!"

She was leaning close to me now. Way close. Pushing her face into mine.

Where was Stacey when I needed her? She's good at telling people off. Much better than I am.

Ding!

The lift door opened. I darted out.

Jacqui's room was on the next floor. But she followed me out.

"Are you lying to me, Robert?" she called out.

"About what?" I said over my shoulder.

"About Stacey. You still like her, don't you? That's why you're so scared of me."

That did it.

I spun around. "I'm not scared of *you*."

"Yeah? Well, let me tell you something,

ROBERT

Robert Brewster. Stacey has, like, totally deaded you."

"Really? She told you, or did you just read her mind?"

"It's so obvious, Robert. Everyone sees it except you."

That did it. I was not going to take this.

"I know exactly how Stacey feels, Jacqui. You sure don't. I don't mean to shock you, but it's possible for a guy and girl to be friends after they break up."

"Then why — I mean, if you're not going with her —?"

"What makes you think I want *you* to be my girlfriend?"

Jacqui's face tightened. "Okay. Fine. You don't have to yell at me."

I felt like a jerk. I *was* yelling at her.

"I'm sorry," I said. "Look, I don't mean to be harsh. I guess I just don't want to have a girlfriend right now, that's all. No offense."

"Okay," Jacqui said, turning back toward the lift. "No problem."

I felt a little guilty watching her go.

But not *too* guilty.

Later on that day, I told Stacey what had happened.

She was cool. She said Jacqui deserved it.

She also said, "I'm really glad you did this on your own, Robert."

At first I thought that was kind of a put-down.

But Stacey didn't mean it that way.

To tell the truth, I agreed with her.

CHAPTER 12

Dawn

Thursday

This is so weird.

Janine had to come to our camp because we needed a last-minute head counselor. To do that, she had to quit her job at another camp, the Sunshine Gang Day Camp.

Sunshine Gang hired someone else. But THAT person is sick today. So now Sunshine Gang needs someone.

Dawn

Of course, Janine's
going over to help, right?
    Wrong. Ms. Garcia
won't let her take the
day off.
    So guess who's going
there?
    Me.

Dawn

"Let me go," Claudia said.

Janine shook her head. "I've already told them that Dawn is going."

"It's okay if Claudia goes in my place," I said.

"It'll be a great experience," Claudia insisted.

"The children here are looking forward to the Nature Art Project," Janine said. "That was your idea, Claudia, and you're the only one with the expertise to pull it off. As your head counselor, I cannot let you go."

End of conversation. Janine walked off, clipboard in hand.

I thought Claudia was going to throw a tube of paint at her.

"Of course I can't go," Claudia muttered. "Janine needs someone to torture."

"Sorry," I said. "I tried."

Claudia was angrily slamming down her art supplies on a table. "It's not your fault that I'm stuck here with Sister Godzilla."

Poor Claudia.

Janine had been like Jekyll and Hyde. Fine to the kids. Fine to the counselors. But very hard on Claudia.

I signaled Mary Anne to come and help out. Then I scooted away.

The truth? I was excited about going to the Sunshine Gang Day Camp. I've always wanted to learn more about working with special-needs children.

In Palo City, where I live, I often baby-sit for a girl who has Down Syndrome, Whitney Cater. Down Syndrome is a form of retardation. (Kids with this condition are pretty easily recognizable. They have round faces and narrow eyes. Often they also have unusually sweet personalities.)

Whitney is an absolute doll.

I could use my experience with her at the new camp.

I walked the half mile or so to Stoneybrook Day School, where the camp was located. As I approached the playground, I could see a group of counselors leading kids out of the building. A couple of the kids appeared to have Down Syndrome, but most didn't. Many of them ran around gleefully, but some were in wheelchairs and others had difficulty walking.

Among them, holding a clipboard and wearing a big whistle, was an energetic-looking woman with long brown hair and a trim, runner's physique.

She smiled and waved me to her. "You must be Dawn! I'm Lila Schwartz. I can't thank you enough for coming to help."

A loud scream from behind her nearly made me jump.

Dawn

Ms. Schwartz turned casually around to look. "That's William," she said. "He does that when he's very happy. Janine *did* tell you what kind of camp this is?"

"Yes," I replied. "Sort of."

"Some of our children have limited mobility," Ms. Schwartz said. "Cerebral palsy, congenital birth malformations, and so on. Others have rather severe developmental issues — Down Syndrome or various degrees of retardation. We have a child who is an autistic savant. . . ."

I knew that term. It described a girl named Susan Felder, for whom Kristy used to baby-sit.

An autistic person has difficulty communicating with other people. A savant is someone with an exceptional talent. Susan, according to Kristy, was a great piano player. If you played a song for her — on tape, from the radio, anything — she played it back perfectly. If you sang a lyric, she repeated it, word for word.

But she didn't talk at all.

When I asked if the girl was Susan, Ms. Schwartz's face brightened. "Good, you know her! Susan amazes us. She's only here for a short while, though. She goes to a special school, year-round, but it closes each summer for a week. She's with the indoor children. I was going to ask you to help with them anyway."

"I'd love to," I said.

Ms. Schwartz gave me some forms to sign. As she led me toward the building, she introduced me to some of the counselors.

On the playground, several kids in wheelchairs were playing half-court basketball. A loud, laugh-filled volleyball game was underway. I saw bubble making, medicine-ball games, sand play, and a group singalong.

The counselor-to-camper ratio looked about one to three. No one was sitting around unattended.

I was impressed.

"Most of the indoor children are in the gymnasium," Ms. Schwartz explained. "Unfortunately the noise level doesn't suit some of them, including Susan."

As we turned the corridor toward the gym, I heard some classical piano music. It was coming from a small room at the end of the hallway.

The door was ajar. Ms. Schwartz waited for the tune to end, then pushed the door open further.

"Susan," she said, "this is Dawn Schafer."

Susan was sitting at the piano, her hands resting in her lap.

She didn't even look at me.

Ms. Schwartz filled me in on Susan's eating schedule, some of her habits. "Susan can be left here while she's playing. I need you to help in

the gym, but do keep an eye on this room," she said. "If you see Susan leave, please make sure someone goes with her. Chances are she'll head for Room Two Hundred, the coach's room. We've set up her machine there, but the door's locked, so you have to get the key from Heather, our head counselor."

"Machine?"

"It has made a world of difference. Susan can't take close human contact. A hug, to her, feels like being swallowed up by a swarm of bees. But when the comfort comes from a machine, somehow it's more calming. The system was developed by an autistic woman who became a college professor."

"Cool," I said cheerfully.

The moment Ms. Schwartz left, Susan stood up. I figured she might want to leave, so I stuck around. But all she did was pace across the room, wringing her hands and making clicking noises with her mouth.

"Am I making you nervous?" I asked.

Flap, flap, click.

"I really loved your playing," I went on. "You can keep going, if you want."

Flap, click, click.

"Of course, you don't have to . . ."

Susan turned suddenly and left the room.

I followed her into the hallway. She walked

127

straight to Room 200 and stood there, facing the door.

"Do you want to go in?" I asked.

It was as if no one had said a word.

I knew I needed to be patient. I've always been patient with Whitney whenever she's done unexpected things.

But Susan wasn't at all like Whitney. Whitney at least had a smile for you. She answered you when you spoke to her. She joked around.

I sighed. "Okay, okay, I'll be right back."

I ran into the gym, found Heather, and introduced myself. Then I got the key from her and ran back into the hallway. Susan was standing in exactly the same place.

I opened the door. Inside, the coach's desk had been pushed against the wall, along with lots of sports equipment.

In the center of the room was a big, padded apparatus that looked like some weird weight machine.

Susan walked inside it. She wedged herself between thick pads that went from her shoulders to her ankles.

Then she pressed a button, and the pads began to close around her. Like a giant hand.

"Susan?"

I was scared. I thought she was going to be hurt.

"Ms. Schwartz!" I called down the hallway, hoping she'd hear. *"Ms. Schwartz!"*

Ms. Schwartz came running into the room. "What happened?"

"Is this — okay?" I gestured toward the room.

All I could see of Susan was her head, poking out from the top of the machine.

"I'm sorry, I thought you understood," Ms. Schwartz said softly. "It's a hug machine, Dawn."

Soon the machine let go. Susan backed out, then turned and walked toward us.

She still didn't say anything. She still didn't look into our eyes. She walked by us and continued to the piano room.

But her hands weren't flapping. And her tongue wasn't clicking. She seemed very peaceful.

Ms. Schwartz sighed. "Yesterday she looked at me. Just for a second. It made my whole day."

The piano playing started again. Ms. Schwartz put an arm around my shoulder as we walked toward the gym.

"Are a lot of the kids here like Susan?" I asked.

A sudden angry cry rang out from the basketball court.

I looked in to see four boys piling onto a ball

under the hoop. And a couple of counselors try-ing to help.

"For some," Ms. Schwartz said with a smile, "physical contact is not a problem."

"Sammy, no biting!" one of the counselors yelled.

Ms. Schwartz ran inside, blowing her whistle.

I followed.

I had work to do.

CHAPTER 13

Mallory

Private Journal
A dream

The blackness outside my window is changing to gray. The air seems thick, almost liquid. A tiny screech breaks the stillness, and I watch the flight of a bird, which seems to have sprung to life from the gnarled branch of a tree.

I turn to my desk and try to write. But I can't. My fingers won't move. My heroine, Mariel, is stuck in her story. And I can't do anything about it.

I hear footsteps outside my room. I jump into bed. My foot catches the

131

chair, and the chair falls to the floor with a thud.

"Mallory?" a familiar voice calls out. "Do you know what time it is?"

"Sorry," I reply from under my blanket.

A silhouette in nightcap and nightclothes picks up the pages of my story. As a light flickers on, I see that my room has been transformed. My desk lamp has become a candle. A quill pen rests in an inkwell where my electric pencil sharpener used to be.

Dad is wearing a nightcap and a thick flannel robe. In the candlelight, with his back to me, he begins to read.

"It's good work, my dear," he finally says, his voice soft and gentle. "Very good."

He lifts the candle. Still holding my story, he walks toward me and sits at the edge of my bed. "Perhaps we can discuss ways to develop the plot...."

In the flickering amber light, I see his face. His high forehead and pencil-thin beard.

My dad has become William Shakespeare....

132

"I thought you were having a heart attack," Jessi said. "Pass the crumpets, please."

"Sorry, I didn't mean to scream." I handed the pastry plate to Jessi across the breakfast table. "The dream was just so weird."

"You have Shakespeare on the brain," Stacey remarked.

"I would too if I found out he was one of *my* ancestors," Abby said.

Kristy swallowed a bite of scrambled egg and nodded. "I know how she feels. I'm distantly descended from Wally Pipp."

"Who?" we all said at once.

"The great Yankee hitter who led the American League in home runs and RBIs in 1916," she said.

Stacey slapped her forehead. "Oh, *that* Wally Pipp."

Kristy threw a crumpet at her.

My friends' good moods were rubbing off on me. Abby was even more up than usual, because she was going to visit the Queen with Victoria. Stacey was thrilled because (a) she finally had her suitcase, (b) she and Kristy were about to take a tour that included shopping, and (c) she had realized that having her mom and Robert along on the trip wasn't so bad after all.

I was feeling pretty happy too. I'd convinced

Mr. D to take a group of us to Stratford-upon-Avon, Shakespeare's birthplace. I'd also called Gillian, and she had agreed to meet us there.

"Take that family-tree book with you today, Mal," Kristy suggested. "If you present it, they might give you free admission."

Abby nodded. "Just say, 'Member of the family.'"

"Guys, don't go overboard," I said. "We're not *that* closely related. Shakespeare lived over four hundred years ago."

Stacey took a pencil from her pack and began scribbling on a napkin. "Let's see ... figure twenty-five years per generation, that makes approximately seventeen generations. Now, you have two parents, four grandparents, eight great-grandparents ... it's exponential, see? So going back as far as Shakespeare, who is your great-times-seventeen grandparent, we figure two to the seventeenth power ..."

Stacey's fingers were flying.

"Did you get that?" Abby asked.

Kristy shook her head. "I'm descended from jocks, not geniuses."

"How many great-times-seventeen grandparents did I have?" I asked.

"One hundred thirty-one thousand seventy-two," Stacey replied.

136

"So I have one one-hundred-thirty-one-thousandths of Shakespeare's genes?" I asked.

"More or less," Stacey said.

I shrugged. "I guess that's why I'm having trouble writing stories these days. Not enough Will in my blood."

"Maybe you need to immerse yourself in him," Abby said, suddenly standing up. "We can help. Ahem. Mayest I fetcheth thou some juice from yonder machine?"

As Abby turned, her smile faded. Michel was heading for our table, carrying his breakfast tray.

"Zounds, methinks I sighteth the enemy," she murmured.

Kristy grimaced.

"Mind if I join you?" Michel asked.

"Yes," said Kristy.

Michel sat down next to her. "And good morning to you too."

"This seat's saved," Kristy said.

"For whom?" Michel asked.

"Anyone but you."

"Fine. I'll switch seats with your boyfriend. OH, ALAAAANNN . . ."

"Don't you even think of it, Michel!" Kristy shot back.

"Ah, *now* you don't mind." Michel grinned

and pulled a harmonica out of his back pocket. "You know what I learned last night?"

"Put that away before I make you eat it!" Kristy said.

Jessi and I exchanged a *time-to-go* Look. We stood up, said good-bye, and returned our trays.

Then, back up to our room, where I made sure to pack a paperback copy of *Romeo and Juliet* I'd bought. (That's what was playing at the Royal Shakespeare Company. Mr. D had said he'd try to get us tickets.)

Our group was waiting for us in the lobby — six more students, half from SMS and half from Berger. As usual, the two groups were sticking to themselves.

"Friends, Canadians, and countrymen!" Mr. D announced. "We're all here, so . . . tallyho!"

"Is he like this all the time?" asked one of the Berger students, a girl named Frances.

"Only in England," I replied.

Mr. D led us into the tube and we promptly went in the wrong direction. We just barely made our connection to the rail train at Paddington Station.

The ride itself took a good two hours. On the way, Mr. D suggested that we read aloud from *Romeo and Juliet*. Which turned out to be fun.

The Berger kids were pretty cool. For the first

time, we were all talking together, getting to know each other. I did not, however, tell them about my ancestry. I didn't want them to treat me like a celebrity or anything.

Gillian was waiting for us at the Stratford-upon-Avon station. "Welcome home, O daughter of the Bard!" she called out.

Thank you, Gillian.

Oh, well, no one seemed to know what she meant.

How was Stratford-upon-Avon? Fantastic. Like taking a time trip. The houses look exactly the way they did in the fifteen hundreds — low, Tudor-style buildings with thatched roofs on narrow, cobbled streets.

As we walked, I imagined living there, dressed in frilly Elizabethan clothes, going home to . . .

The Shakespeare birthplace! It still exists.

Well, that's not totally true. It's been rebuilt, and it's now called the Shakespeare Centre. But some of the original beams are still standing. I touched one of them while no one was looking.

Great-times-seventeen-grandpa Will's grave is still there too. (That was *not* rebuilt.) I stood there for awhile after everyone had left. I tried to contact Will's spirit. I asked it to help me finish my story.

I felt ridiculous.

That evening we almost missed seeing *Romeo*

and Juliet. Mr. D had forgotten to call for tickets in advance. He assumed we'd just pick some up at the box office, but the show was sold out. (Luckily Gillian knew how to stick around to get last-minute cancellations. Our group's seats were scattered throughout the theater, but I managed to sit with Gillian and Jessi.)

The performance blew me away. Coming from the mouths of the English actors, the words don't sound old-fashioned at all. They make everything as clear and natural as today. I was weeping by the end, and so were Gillian and Jessi.

All the way back to London, I thought about scenes from the play.

I also thought about something else. An incident that had happened earlier, at a place we'd visited right after seeing Shakespeare's grave.

The house was called Hall's Croft. Shakespeare's daughter, Susanna, had lived there.

As we walked through one of the smaller rooms, Jessi let out a gasp. "Oh my lord . . . look at that painting."

My cousin and I stopped to look.

The small oil portrait of Susanna desperately needed a cleaning. But the face peering through the grime was familiar.

It wasn't an exact likeness. The hair color was off, and the face was a little too round.

But something about the expression was unmistakable.

"Do you see it too?" Jessi asked.

We nodded. None of us had to say a word.

Susanna looked a lot like Gillian.

A funny thing happened that night. My mind was racing around, long after Jessi fell asleep. I couldn't stop thinking about that painting.

The resemblance haunted me. It *had* to be a coincidence. A hundred-thirty-one-thousandth of a gene couldn't possibly show in a person's face.

Or could it?

I tried to take my mind off it. I thought about our trip to France, which was scheduled for the next day. I thought about my family and friends back home, about the story I couldn't finish . . .

Zing. Wide-awake again.

Have I described my story? It already had a title: "If Life Is a Barrel of Monkeys, I Must Be a Banana." It was about a girl going totally nuts because her parents expect too much of her, her brothers and sisters tease her, and her best friend moves to New York City.

Mr. D always says, "Write what you know." I figured I'd take a familiar situation and make a funny, realistic story out of it. Like Judy Blume or Judith Viorst. But I was stuck. The story was just too close to my life, and I sure didn't find it funny. Whenever I tried to write, I saw a big, blank wall.

But now, for some reason, the answer seemed clear.

Forget about realism.

What if the girl has gone to sleep and wakes up in another time? Even better, what if she's switched places with someone famous — like Shakespeare's daughter — and no one knows the difference?

The blank wall was dissolving. I could visualize characters. And they were moving. Interacting. Reacting to one another.

I wondered if Grandpa Will saw his plays like this.

I climbed out of bed. Quietly I turned on the desk lamp and pulled my story from a drawer.

First of all, I'd have to change the title, but that could wait. I could think of a better one later.

I grabbed a pen and started writing.

CHAPTER 14

Kristy

Friday

I think Ms. McGill is cool.
I don't care what Stacey says.
Today's our last full day here,
so she told us to pick things
we'd regret not doing if we left
without doing them. Stacey, of
course, wanted to go shopping
(in this place called Soho). I
wanted to see a cricket match.
Hey, since England has no
baseball stadiums, why not
check out their version?
I thought Stacey was going to
kill me.
But her mom said yes. To both

143

Kristy

of us. (A Berger group is coming along too, with their chaperone. Kind of a joint venture.)

So next time I see you guys, I'll teach you how to play a new sport! I can't wait.

I wonder if they have hot dogs at the stadium....

"McGill . . . Thomas . . . Smith . . ."

As Ms. McGill read off the names of the students going on our trip, kids shouted out "Here."

I was itching to leave. Breakfast had been such a pain. I had indigestion because Michel was sitting next to me. And he actually tried to play his *harmonica*. Can you believe it?

"Faure . . . DuMoulin?" shouted the Berger chaperone, Mr. Brown.

My jaw went *thunk* as it hit the Persian rug.

"Here I am!" cried a voice from behind me. It sounded like fingernails on a blackboard.

"Forget about cricket, I'm going with Mal's group!" I blurted out.

"They left already," Stacey said. "So did the other group."

"But — but I can't go with *him*!"

"Oh, behave," Michel shot back. "I knew you'd be in this group too, but I expressed my disgust privately."

"That's easy for you to do," I replied. "You have to look in the mirror every morning."

"Kristyyyyy," Ms. McGill warned.

Okay. Time to flip into emergency survival mode.

I walked straight to Stacey, who was close to

the hotel entrance. "Keep your body between mine and his at all times."

"Kristy, please," Stacey said wearily. "Just kiss him and put both of you out of your misery."

"I won't dignify that with an answer," I answered.

I did not find her comment amusing.

Lord's Cricket Ground was close to our hotel, so we walked. I was careful to keep Stacey between me and Michel. Like a shield.

Whenever he came near me, he pulled out his harmonica and started playing songs. "Take Me Out to the Ballgame." The Canadian national anthem. Plus a song I only vaguely recognized.

"What's that?" I asked.

"'Michelle,'" he replied. "The *girl's* name. It's an old Beatles song."

Is that weird or what?

When we reached the stadium, I sat between Stacey and her mom.

Michel sat right behind me.

"Why is he doing this?" I hissed to Stacey.

"Just enjoy the game," she replied. "We're sacrificing prime shopping time for this."

But I couldn't concentrate. One, because Michel kept shouting, "Go, Blue Jays."

And two, because cricket wasn't at all what I'd expected.

146

It's like baseball designed by a golfer. Some of the same rules, but seventeen times as boring. No diving catches, no stolen bases, no power pitchers. Plus, the players keep changing sides all the time for no reason.

"Are you following this?" Stacey asked at one point.

"Whose idea was this anyway?" Michel piped up.

"Okay, okay," I said. "I made a mistake."

Michel shrugged. "I was going to *thank* you. I'm enjoying this."

Figures.

"If you stay for a whole match," said a white-haired man sitting near Michel, "you can become quite addicted."

"How long does a match last?" Ms. McGill asked.

"Until sundown," the man replied. "With a break for tea, of course."

Sundown?

My addiction would just have to start another year.

We snuck out quickly.

Our next stop: Soho, Stacey's idea of heaven. Basically, it's wall-to-wall shops and restaurants.

Ms. McGill and Mr. Brown divided us into two groups: Boutique and non-boutique. Guess which one Michel chose?

Kristy

Which meant I was stuck boutique-hopping with Stacey and her mom.

To me, this is a fate worse than cricket. I have an allergy to boutiques. I become like Dorothy in the poppy field: zzzzzzz.

I couldn't take it for very long. When I spotted the other group ducking into a place called the London Kite and Juggling Company, I had to follow them.

Michel didn't notice me until I was at the cashier, paying for a beginning juggler's set.

"You know how to juggle?" he asked.

"I'll learn," I said, walking out to the sidewalk.

"Let me show you." He took the package out of my hand and started ripping it open. "It's all in the rhythm. . . ."

"Give that to me!" I grabbed it back.

The four balls spilled out onto the sidewalk and bounced away.

I ran after them. So did Michel.

We ran patterns around the pedestrians. Michel nearly knocked over an old lady. I made a lightning-quick save to keep a ball from rolling into the sewer.

By the time we reached the end of the block, I had one juggling ball and Michel had two.

We were out of breath. People were staring at us. I felt like an idiot.

"Excuse me?" A very proper woman was walking toward us, pulling a golden retriever behind her. "Is this yours?"

She held out one of the juggling balls. It had a bite mark on it and was still wet with dog drool.

"It's his," I said.

The woman dropped it into Michel's hand. He looked ready to barf.

It was about the funniest thing I'd seen all week. I burst out laughing.

Michel scowled at me. Then he began laughing too.

What a shock. An actual sense of humor.

For a tiny moment I thought he might be human.

Then he threw the slimed ball at me.

And I, of course, caught it. By instinct.

"You creep!" I yelled.

Michel was off like a rocket.

I wanted to kill him.

CHAPTER 15

Abby

TRAVEL REPORT
Dateline: Friday.
London, England.
Correspondent: A.S.
Today we visited
my namesake.
Westminster Abbey.
I wanted to
tell them they spelled
Abby wrong.
My newest friend.
Darcy Boynton, told
me not to sweat it.
(She's from Bergere.
I mean, Berger.)
To tell you the

truth, I don't remember much about W.A. Except that it was big.

Oh, one other thing. Darcy saved my life.

But that's another story....

Abby

Kristy is such a slave driver. She said I *had* to write that report, because I was the only BSC member in my group's day trip, and if I didn't write anything, Claudia, Mary Anne, Dawn, Logan, and Shannon wouldn't have a complete and accurate account of our European vacation, and what a tragedy that would be.

Frankly, I had other things on my mind during the day. This poem, for instance:

> *Abigail, Abigail, where have you been?*
> *I've been to London to visit the Queen.*
> *Abigail, Abigail, what did you there?*
> *I frightened her senseless because of my hair.*

Yes, this was THE DAY. The most important event of the trip — maybe of my whole life — was scheduled for four o'clock. I had a responsibility. I was an ambassador. I was representing America the Beautiful.

Sure.

My hair was a mountain majesty. I believe starlings were nesting in it.

My face was a fruited plain. Zits galore. A pimple on my left cheek the size of a kumquat.

I couldn't even get past number 1 on my Checklist for Meeting the Queen — "Avoid scaring her . . ."

The Queen was going to take one look and faint. I could just see the tabloid headline describing me: *"Abbus Horribilis,* the Monster of Buckingham Palace!"

Poor Darcy. She had to listen to my complaints during the entire trip. I don't know why she didn't ditch me.

"Why don't you just get a haircut?" she finally said.

Duh.

Why hadn't I thought of that?

I told Mr. LaVigne and Mr. Brown about my dilemma. They let me duck into a hairstylist after we left Westminster Abbey, while the others shopped nearby. (That, by the way, is how Darcy saved my life.)

Personally, I hope we stay in touch with the Berger kids. They are pretty cool.

Okay, back to the good stuff.

Cut to three o'clock. In front of the Cardington Inn. Waiting for Victoria's driver.

My hair was fine. My pimple was buried under makeup. Darcy, my lady-in-waiting-for-the-afternoon, was holding my hand.

Which was shaking.

"I can't do this," I said. "I mean, what do I *say*? 'Greetings, Your Highness'? 'Hello, Queen'? 'At your service, my liege'? What's a liege, anyway?"

"Look, Abby, just be natural."

" 'Yo, what's up, my lady?' "

"Well . . ."

Too late. Victoria's driver was pulling up.

I hugged Darcy, squealed a good-bye, and climbed into the car.

The driver looked like a friendly guy. So I asked him, "Excuse me, what do you say when you meet the Queen?"

He laughed. "Can't say as I've ever had the pleasure. I imagine it doesn't really matter. As long as you keep it clean."

Clean.

My teeth. I hadn't brushed them since breakfast. Yikes!

"Do you have any mints or gum?" I asked.

He reached into his pocket and gave me a stick of gum.

We drove up to the gates of Buckingham Palace (yes, *THE*). Victoria's driver gave the guard some official papers, announcing: "Kent, guest, for the Queen's reception."

My heart was acting like a prisoner in the Tower of London, banging against the walls. I had to hold my hand against it. I was afraid it would escape.

We parked. As we climbed out, I spotted Miss Rutherford among a throng of people. She was busily fixing the bow on Victoria's white tulle dress.

Everyone was so elegantly dressed. Victoria looked gorgeous. Her hair was arranged in an elegant French braid. She was wearing white gloves and carrying a basket full of flowers.

I drew myself up straight and walked regally forward.

Chomp-chomp-chomp, went my mouth.

Oops.

I swallowed the gum.

"You've arrived at last," Miss Rutherford remarked.

"Thank goodness!" Victoria said. "Now maybe Miss Rutherford will stop fussing."

I tried to make conversation. But I was so nervous, I might as well have been speaking Albanian. Plus, I could feel my allergies kicking in, because of all the flowers.

Finally I managed to ask, "Where should I stadd?"

Great. My nose was stopped up. I was going to sound like Elmer Fudd. Hewwo, you scwewy Queen.

"Behind me, of course," Victoria said. "Miss Rutherford will stand behind you if her ankles hold up. Then she can fuss with *your* clothing."

"And what should I —"

Say, would have been the next word out of my mouth. But I was interrupted.

"Flower girls, please step up!" a voice called out.

This was it.

I took a deep breath.

"Pleased to beet you, Your Bajesty," I murmured under my breath.

"Excuse me?" Miss Rutherford said.

"Just practicigg," I replied.

I wiped my sweaty palms on my nice dress and followed Victoria.

A railing had been set up a few yards back from the winding driveway. Victoria walked toward it, along with other little flower girls in stunning outfits.

Lots of little flower girls. At least two dozen.

"Are they *all* pridcesses?" I asked.

Victoria laughed. "Of course not, silly."

I followed Victoria as she ducked under the railing. The other girls were lining up along the road. I figured Victoria would be led somewhere special. To the first-class section. The princesses' area. Whatever.

But she just took her place along the road with all the other girls.

Suddenly I had the feeling everyone was staring at me.

"Abigail!" Miss Rutherford's voice called out.

"Stand back, please!" barked a guard, who gestured toward the railing.

Miss Rutherford was standing behind it. So were all the other adults.

Ugh. I ran back to it and ducked under.

"This . . . this is it?" I asked Miss Rutherford. "I thought — ared't we goigg to greet the Queed persodally, sidce we're Victoria's guests?"

Miss Rutherford let out a hooty little chuckle. "Oh, dear, no. Is that what Victoria told you? If the Queen met all the guests of the flower girls, she'd be here all day. This is merely a ceremony, you see. These are the daughters of the various ambassadors and politicians who have organized this event, of course."

"Oh."

I smiled. I did not look heartbroken.

Now people were crowding closer to the rail. I craned my neck to see a motorcade rolling slowly up the winding driveway.

It stopped by the front of the palace. A group of people emerged from the cars and climbed the stairs, followed by the flower girls.

Then I saw her. The Queen!

She was smaller than I had imagined. Even so, just *seeing* her brought a lump to my throat.

She was escorted by a guy I recognized. Prince Something. I forget. He's been on the news. The flower girls followed closely behind.

Abby

The Queen turned and waved to the crowd.

Then, one by one, the girls presented the flowers. Actually, a woman next to the Queen accepted the bouquets while the girls curtsied. The Queen smiled at each girl, patting a few of them on the head.

Victoria was beaming as she stepped up to the Queen. Her curtsy was perfect, and the Queen said something to her that made her smile.

I heard a little, choked-back gasp from Miss Rutherford.

When I turned to face her, she was wiping away a tear.

I have to admit, my eyes were soggy too. I guess People of Extreme Fame bring that out. (I hear Elvis had that effect.)

Soon the Queen ducked inside, and we guests were allowed past the railing.

Several people from the motorcade were still milling around, organizing themselves into groups for an official-looking photographer.

Miss Rutherford and I began walking up the steps.

"Vicki!" I called out.

Victoria turned. I'd never seen her smile so widely. "Abigail! Come! I have to tell you what happened!"

I ran toward her. Dodging the crowd. Skipping up and down the steps.

I didn't see the man to my left until I was on top of him.

Literally. I stepped right on his wingtip shoes.

"Oh! Sorry!" I cried out.

I looked up.

Glaring down at me was . . . him.

The Prince.

The one who'd been escorting the Queen.

My mouth fell open.

Click! went the court photographer's camera.

"Quite all right," said the Prince.

And just like that, he was off.

Leaving me in total shock.

I, Abby Stevenson, had stepped on Royal Toes.

I looked at my shoes. Were they glowing, or was that my imagination?

Victoria had been watching the scene. She was laughing. "Abigail, do you know who that is? You must get that photograph!"

I looked around for the photographer. But he was gone too.

I never did find out what the Queen had said to Vicki. Frankly, I was obsessed about something else.

I knew I had to find that photo.

Otherwise no one would believe what happened.

CHAPTER 16

Claudia

Friday

The end of the week at SES Playground camp!

I'm about to leve home. Janine's probly going to start yelling at me any minut.

In case you were wondering, Thursday was just fine. Exept that Ms Garcia did not fire Coky. (To bad.) Oh well, Matthew H didnt' catch newmonia, thats the good news.

Uh oh, there goes Janine. She just yelled at me.

Yes mam. Eye- eye mam. Whatever you say mam.

Got to go.

"What's a laggard?" I asked.

Dawn was emerging from the SES equipment shed, carrying jump ropes and dodgeballs. "I don't know. Some kind of drink?"

"That's what Janine called me this morning," I said.

As Mary Anne and I rummaged around for traffic cones, Logan picked up a crate full of sports equipment. "Janine called you a drink?" he asked.

"I think *laggard* means 'slowpoke,'" Mary Anne said.

"Great," I said. "She can't just *say* slowpoke. She can't just diss me to my face. She has to give me a delayed-reaction insult."

Mary Anne and I walked across the field and began setting up relay-race lanes.

"I thought camp would loosen her up," I grumbled, "but no-o-o-o."

"Don't you think she's improving?" Mary Anne asked. "I do. Look at her now."

I glanced toward the school building. Janine was sitting at a picnic table. She was surrounded by laughing, happy campers. They all seemed excited about something she was showing them.

I nearly fainted at the sight. Was this *my* sister, Janine the Kid-Challenged?

"Well," I said, "she's still impossible to me."

Out of the corner of my eye, I could see Jerry heading over to Janine. He looked angry.

Out of the *other* corner of my eye I spotted a red object heading for me.

I ducked in the nick of time, and it whizzed over my head.

"Ohhhhh, I am *such* a klutz!" whined the voice of Cokie Mason.

The red thing — a soft, football-shaped object with a plastic foam arrow-tail attached to it — was lying on the ground to my right.

Logan's campers were howling with laughter. Cokie was with them, giggling hysterically.

I could feel Mary Anne tense up. She knows that Cokie has a wicked crush on Logan. He has zero interest in her, and he's told her that. But she never gives up.

Even when Mary Anne is around.

"Claudia, could you toss that back?" Logan asked.

"Me?" I squeaked.

Oh, wonderful. I'm bad enough throwing regular balls. I wouldn't know how to *hold* this thing.

"It's a Vortex!" Logan said, as if that explained everything.

"*Anyone* can throw it!" shouted eight-year-old Jake Kuhn.

162

I swallowed hard.

I picked up the thing, reared back, and threw.

You know what? Logan was right. I threw a perfect spiral (I think that's what you call it). It didn't go anywhere near him, but it was beautiful to watch.

"Yeeaaaa!" I cheered.

"Go, Claudia!" yelled Buddy Barrett.

"Are you having *fun*?"

Janine's sarcastic voice sent an icy chill up my spine.

She was stalking toward me, scowling.

"I was just —" I began.

"You're supposed to be setting up for the races!"

"Janine! Catch!" Logan shouted.

The Vortex came hurtling our way again.

Janine let out a yelp of surprise and ducked away.

Logan was cracking up. Of course, Cokie was too. I thought Janine was going to kill them.

She didn't.

She dumped on me.

"You see what you've started, Claudia?"

"*I* didn't do anything!" I said.

"It's your *example*," Janine replied. "You set the tone. If you permit chaos, it grows. Just like the mess in your room."

"What does *my room* have to do with this?"

"It's a simile, Claudia. Do I need to spell it out, or can you do the mental work yourself?"

Enough.

I had had enough of being picked on.

Enough of similes and laggards and words I didn't understand.

Enough of being made to feel like a stupid, worthless little sister in front of my friends.

"You love to show off, huh?" I said. "It makes you feel *so good.*"

Janine let out an exasperated sigh. "That's beside the point —"

"No, Janine. It's beside *your* point. This may be hard for you to believe, but *I* have a point too. You have been on my back all week. Why? Because I know how to have fun? Because kids like me? Is that it, Janine? You're jealous?"

"Claudiaaa," Mary Anne said softly.

"Look, guys," Logan added, "it was my fault, okay? I'm sorry about the Vortex —"

"No," I interrupted. "I have something to say and I'm not going to —"

"I don't need to hear another word!"

I have never heard Janine yell like that. Her face was all red. She looked as if she wanted to cry.

A group of campers turned around to look at her. Dawn came running to us. "Is everything all right?"

164

"Fine, Dawn." Janine swallowed hard and collected herself. "Sorry for that outburst. Claudia, I am perfectly capable of understanding another point of view. You do not need to remind me of my shortcomings. I have ample reminders every day, all day."

With that, she turned and left.

"What did she mean by that?" Logan asked.

"I have no idea," I replied.

I should have been happy. I'd said what was on my mind. I'd finally given Janine a taste of her own medicine.

But I felt awful.

I turned to set up the finish line for the relay races.

Out of the corner of my eye, I watched Janine. She was gathering up a pile of cards from the picnic table where she'd been sitting earlier.

She caught my glance. I thought I could see moisture in her eyes.

Oh, great.

This was too much.

I'd done exactly what I'd accused her of doing. Insulted her in front of everyone.

"Can you guys cover for me?" I asked.

"Sure," said Mary Anne.

I ran toward my sister. I caught up with her just outside the door to the gym. "Janine? Look, I didn't mean to yell at you."

"Yes you did."

"Well, okay, I did. But —"

"But I deserved it."

The words froze in my throat.

That was not the reply I'd expected.

Janine was looking at the ground. "I suppose you know it has not been an easy week for me, Claudia. But Jerry's behavior is no excuse for me to take my frustration out on you. I apologize."

"Jerry? What does he have to do with this?"

Janine looked surprised. "Haven't you noticed?"

"Well, no. I've been so busy —"

"He's been overbearing, Claudia. He has so much more experience than I do, and I can't seem to catch on."

"You were doing fine a little while ago."

Janine exhaled. "*I* thought so. I'd set up a math contest for the campers — you know, weird, fun problems. Like a game show. I worked all last night on the concept. And the kids were loving it. But Jerry told me to pack it up."

"Why?"

"Not appropriate. He said, 'This is a summer camp, not a college classroom.' But that's how I *relate* to kids. I tutor them. I get them interested in math and science."

"They were having fun. *That's* appropriate."

"He's been saying things like that all week, Claudia. I feel as though I can't do anything right. So I try harder and harder. And it doesn't seem to matter. He just chides me even more."

"No wonder you've been so . . ." I let my voice drift off.

"*Mean.* You can say it. I've been too spineless to talk back to Jerry. So my frustration bottles up inside. And it has to go somewhere, so I send it to the safest person. The only person I . . ."

She grew silent. I thought I knew what she wanted to say. I also knew she wouldn't say it.

So I finished her sentence for her. ". . . love?"

Janine nodded. "I was going to say 'trust.' But, yes, that too."

I put my arm around my sister's shoulder. "Janine, will you take some advice from me?"

"It depends," Janine replied.

"Ignore him. Do things your way. If he doesn't back off, bring Ms. Garcia into it."

"And if that doesn't work?"

"I'll take care of him."

Janine burst out laughing. It was a sound I hadn't heard in a long time. "Wait until after camp, though. To avoid further acrimony."

"Whatever. And Janine?"

"Yes?"

"You're doing a fine job. Except when you yell at me."

Janine gave me a wide smile. "I guess we can't all be perfect."

CHAPTER 17

Jessi

Saturday

Farewell, London! I will never, ever forget you!

I've just finished packing. My suitcase is stuffed. So is my brain — full of memories. This has been the BEST trip, and if I write anymore I'll probably drench the paper with my

Jessi

Oh my lord.
You will not
believe who is
outside!
'Bye.
More later!

I raced out of the hotel. Mallory was right behind me. We both nearly tripped over suitcases. A few early birds were already waiting for our tour bus.

"Tanishaaaaa!" I screamed.

Tanisha threw her arms around me. "I'm so glad you're still here!"

"What — why — ?" Behind her stood several members of the Dance NY company. Grinning at me.

Clarissa Jones was among them, her leg in a cast. So was Yolanda Gordon, her understudy.

And in the midst of them was David Brailsford.

"I called the hotel yesterday," Tanisha said. "You were out, but the reception guy said you were all leaving for France, so we came to say good-bye!"

"And to give you this," Mr. Brailsford said. He held up a pair of golden ballet shoes, mounted on a platform. "For services rendered above and beyond the call of duty."

"For me?" My eyes misted up.

The hotel dining room was emptying. I guess people had seen us, because they started to come outside. I could see Abby, Kristy, Stacey, and Mal, all smiling proudly.

I'm not sure who started applauding. I think

Jessi

it was Kristy. But before long the whole group had joined in.

This felt as good as my curtain call at the Barbican.

Well, *almost*.

"Thanks, guys," I said.

"Congratulations, Jessi!" shouted Ms. Post from the hotel door. "But let's keep in mind that the bus arrives in ten minutes!"

Ten?

Kids were rushing inside. I should have gone with them. But I was bursting with questions. "How did the other performances go?"

"Yolanda was fine by the next day," Tanisha replied. "And Clarissa should recover by September. Now go, before you miss the bus!"

"Okay! 'Bye!" I shouted. "I'll miss you!"

"Hope to see you soon!" Mr. Brailsford called out.

"Me too!" I replied.

I meant it. I hoped he did too.

I dashed to my room with Mallory. I threw the rest of my stuff into my suitcase, neatly tucking in my statuette.

Minutes later, Mallory and I were loading our luggage into the cargo area of the bus, along with Kristy, Abby, and Stacey.

"Is there room in here for mine?" asked Michel from behind us.

"No," Kristy lied.

"Heyyyy, I can take a hint," Michel said, turning away. "I just thought you might need a translator when we reach France. Suit yourself."

"We're not taking the bus *to* France," Kristy said. "Just to Victoria Station. We're catching a *train* that goes through the Chunnel."

"For you and me, Kristy," Michel said over his shoulder, "it will be the Chunnel of Love."

"Ooooooh," someone cried out.

Kids were giggling. Kristy's face was bright red.

"Hmmmm, I guess we know how *he* really feels," Stacey said.

"He's doing that to embarrass me, and you know it!" Kristy retorted.

She climbed into the bus, and the rest of us followed. Except for Abby. She was by the newspaper machines, feeding in coins and pulling out papers.

Just then Ms. McGill came running out of the hotel. "Stacey, did you pack your medicine?"

Stacey peered out of the bus door. "Yes, Mom."

"The outfits I lent you?"

"Yes, Mom."

"The ashes?"

Stacey's face flushed. "Mo-*om*! Do you have to say it so loud?"

"Stacey, please give me an answer. I have a lot

173

to do. If I don't find Mr. Dougherty right now, we're not going anywhere!"

"Oh, groan," Stacey said. "Not again."

"He's at Virginia Woolf's house!" Mallory blurted out.

"What's he doing there?" Boy, was Ms. McGill angry. *"Virginia Woolf is dead!"*

"At breakfast he told us it was the one literary place he missed," Mal explained. "He said he'd be back by now."

Muttering to herself, Ms. McGill stomped back into the hotel.

The two Berger chaperones were already on board.

Mr. LaVigne was standing near the bus driver. "We'll give him fifteen minutes. If he doesn't show, he'll have to book passage himself."

Mal and I found seats near the front, just as Abby bustled in. She held a newspaper open in front of her. "Look! I was right there!"

She showed us a photograph — several stiff-looking people in stiff-looking clothes, smiling stiffly at the camera.

"That's the royal family," Mallory said. "Where are you?"

"There." Abby pointed to a spot in the middle of a column of newsprint to the right of the photo. "Just out of sight."

174

Jessi

"Where's the shot of you attacking the Prince?" Stacey asked.

"I'll get it somehow," Abby said. "You'll see."

The next few minutes were wild. First Mr. Dougherty came huffing and puffing onto the bus, apologizing like crazy. Then Stacey ran off the bus to find her mom. Then Ms. McGill came back, and Kristy had to go find Stacey.

We managed to pull away with everyone. But we cut it very close at the train station.

Ms. Post and Mr. LaVigne were freaking out. They thought we'd forfeit our tickets. You never saw a group of kids rush through a station and board a train so fast.

And what a train — a high-speed special that travels straight from London to Paris in three hours. Mal and I found seats together, directly in front of two Berger girls.

"You're the girl David Brailsford was fussing about?" one of them asked.

"You knew that was David Brailsford?" I said. That was impressive. Not too many kids would recognize him.

"I take dance class," said one of the girls, who had dark brown hair and a friendly smile. "My name's Katheryn Giberson."

"Jessica Ramsey."

"How do you know him? Why did he give you that award?"

175

Jessi

Got an hour? I wanted to ask.

I could see that Mallory was already busy writing her story, in a world of her own. Across the aisle, Abby was leafing through the newspapers, and Stacey was reading her World War II book. Kristy was staring out the window, looking glum. Robert was sitting near the back of the train, sharing a laugh with Pete Black. Mrs. McGill and Mr. Dougherty were in a deep, heated discussion.

I turned to face Katheryn. She looked so eager.

Oh, well. It was going to be a long trip, my friends were busy, and I had lots to tell.

"Let's see," I said. "It started last December. . . ."

CHAPTER 18

Stacey

Saturday

Hello from the Chunnel — the new, improved, underground way to cross the English Channel !

Guys, it is the ultimate ride. It leaves the New York City Metro North tunnels in the dust. It's clean. It's bright. And the Eurostar (that's the name of the train) feels as if it's gliding on a cloud.

They should hire me to write ads! ☺

I am sitting next to Abby right now. She wants to say

Hi, everybody! Before I forget, here's a fund-raising idea for the BSC:

Stacey

an auction of THE
shoe that stepped
on an actual prince's
toes. You may have
seen the photo in
the American
papers. If so, please
save me a

Puh-leeze.

As I was saying, we are about to
enter France. Mom's sitting a few
seats in front of us with Mr. Dougherty.
Fortunately they've both dozed off.
Before that, though, they were arguing.
Well, talking, but in these soft,
agitated voices.

I hope they work something out.
Mr. D has been impossible. If he
flakes out one more time, expect
Mom on the first Concorde flight home.

Which, actually, might not be
so bad. Mom has been impossible
too.

Come to think of it, cancel that last
remark. If Mom left, I'd have to
face Mr. Anderson tomorrow all by
myself. . . .

178

"**Y**ou must be Stacey. Am I ever glad to see you."

He was standing in the doorway of Mom's hotel room. He was old — white-haired and wrinkled — but tall and strong-looking.

Mom grabbed the doorknob and opened the door all the way. "Come in, Mr. Anderson. I'm Maureen McGill. We're so sorry you had to go through this trip without your suitcase!"

"Well, I needed to buy some new clothes anyway," Mr. Anderson said with a chuckle. "Haven't done any shopping since my wife passed away."

It was Sunday. Mom had not taken the Concorde home. In fact, she had the day off from official chaperone duties. (Yup. She'd made Mr. Dougherty feel so guilty on the train, he had insisted on it.) This put her in a good mood for the first time since the trip began.

I was fresh and well-rested too. I *adored* Paris. We hadn't seen much of it — just a walk along the River Seine, dinner at a bistro, and an early night at the hotel — but I was totally, totally in love. Our hotel was brand-new, and every room had a balcony with a view of the Eiffel Tower.

I was looking forward to our meeting with Mr. Anderson. I wanted to ask him a million questions about World War Two.

Stacey

Well, maybe a dozen. Frankly, I couldn't wait to hand over those ashes and go sightseeing.

Mom's hotel room was a suite with a bedroom, a sitting room, and a small kitchen. Mom was busily setting out tea and pastries, which room service had sent up. I followed Mr. Anderson into the sitting room.

I noticed that he limped.

"I'll get your suitcase," Mom said.

I beat her to it.

Mr. Anderson opened the suitcase and lifted out the container of ashes. "Thought you'd lose me, eh, old buddy?" he said with a smile.

He was talking to the can. *Très* weird.

"You must be relieved," Mom said. "I know how important this is to you."

"I wasn't worried," Mr. Anderson said confidently. "If Dennis and I could make it through D-Day at Omaha Beach, we could survive a little luggage mix-up."

I thought about the pictures I had seen of D-Day. The men trudging through the sea with full battle gear. Warships rocking on the water, planes buzzing overhead.

"So . . . you were *in* that?" I asked.

"Hard to believe this feeble old guy could invade France, eh?" Mr. Anderson burst out laughing.

Open mouth, insert foot.

I felt myself turning red. "I meant, it must have been awful. Were you hurt?"

"Nahh, not too bad," Mr. Anderson said. "Dennis and I were lucky. Some of our pals weren't. The invasion didn't go as well as planned, you know. Terrible weather, choppy and treacherous water. Thousands of us had to jump off the troopships in water up to our necks, loaded down with weapons and supplies. The Germans had planted mines. There were craters underwater, from bombs that had fallen. If you stepped in one of those, down you went. For good. Tanks and trucks and jeeps were sticking out of the water, half sunk, their crews trapped inside."

"Thank goodness you made it to shore," Mom said.

"It wasn't much better there," Mr. Anderson said softly. "Gunners were shooting at us from the beach. And if you survived *that*, well, then all you had to do was sweep across a continent and win a war on enemy territory."

He gave a weary, hollow laugh.

I tried to imagine what he had looked like back then. As a young man in a uniform. Dodging enemy fire.

It was impossible.

But he was here to revisit Normandy. Surely he must have brought some mementos.

"Mr. Anderson," I said, "do you have pictures? Of you and your friend, from the war?"

Mr. Anderson reached into his jacket pocket and pulled out a black-and-white photo, worn and yellowed at the edges.

It was a faded image of two men — one blond, with a wide grin; the other dark-haired and movie-star handsome. The blond guy was holding hands with a young woman who looked elated.

"The good-looking guy is Dennis," Mr. Anderson said with a sad smile. "But I'm the one with the beautiful young woman. We were married for fifty-three years before she passed away."

"She's lovely," Mom said.

"This picture was taken at the liberation of Paris, eighty days after Normandy," Mr. Anderson went on. "You know, a lot of the city looks just the same now as it did then."

"In all these years, you haven't come back?" I asked.

"Dennis and I always said we'd make it back to the beach someday," Mr. Anderson said, putting the photo away. "I guess we're finally doing it. I never thought it would be like this, though."

An awkward silence filled the room.

Finally Mr. Anderson stood up. "I don't want

to delay your plans, and I have a long trip ahead of me. Don't know how long it takes to get to Normandy these days. I imagine three hours or so."

"Can I come along?"

The words just jumped out of my mouth. I hadn't even been *thinking* about that.

Mom looked at me as if she were afraid I'd lost my mind.

Mr. Anderson seemed pretty surprised too. "Well, I sure wouldn't mind the company."

"Anastasia McGill," Mom said, raising a skeptical eyebrow, "you want to give up a day of *Paris* in order to go to *Normandy*?"

"I'll have plenty of time in Paris. This is *important*!" It really was. I'd never been so sure of myself.

Mr. Anderson was smiling at Mom. "Of course, I hope that Ms. McGill would come too."

Oh, sure.

Fat chance.

I was kissing the trip good-bye.

Mom took a deep breath. "I'll call Mr. Dougherty," she said. "If he *knows* I won't be around, he'll definitely live up to his promise."

The ride in Mr. Anderson's rented car took exactly three hours. We knew we were close when signs pointed to "The D-Day Beaches at Normandy: Utah, Omaha, Gold, Juno, and Sword." Each beach seemed to have its own monument and museum.

And cars and buses were clogging the access road.

My heart sank. Was this a tourist trap?

But Mr. Anderson followed another sign, to the American cemetery outside Omaha Beach. We stopped to walk inside.

The breath caught in my throat. Nine thousand graves stretched almost to the horizon in perfect lines.

"So many young men," Mom said softly.

"This is less than half of the American deaths during the invasion," Mr. Anderson whispered.

We passed silently among the graves. Mr. Anderson's eyes scanned the names, as if he were looking for friends. He clutched the canister of ashes tightly.

Afterward we walked to the beach itself. The sand was full of tourists, snapping photos and chatting.

Mr. Anderson moved ahead of us, always looking out to sea.

"Stacey." My mom touched my arm.

We both stopped walking.

Mr. Anderson was heading for a section of the beach diagonally to our right. I don't know if he

had recognized the place where he and Dennis had landed, or if it was just a quiet, fairly private spot.

Whatever the reason, he stood there a long time without moving.

Then he carefully took off his shoes and socks, rolled up his pants, and walked into the water.

He must have walked a hundred yards, but when he stopped, the water was only up to his knees.

At that distance, I couldn't see what he was doing.

But when he trudged back, the canister was open.

And empty.

CHAPTER 19

Kristy

Sunday

Ah, Paris!

Home of the croissant. And the baguette. And chocolate mousse.

And frogs' legs and cooked snails.

Très gross, Abby!

Anyway, guys, it's a cool place to eat.

I'll let you know if there's anything much to see....

187

Kristy

"What do you mean, small potatoes?" Michel whined. "It is the largest art museum in the world!"

I hated his accent. I hated the way he always contradicted me. I hated his clothes and his cologne.

But most of all I hated the fact that he would not leave me alone. I couldn't even enjoy the Louvre museum without him tagging along.

"Hey, Stacey has taken me to the Met in New York," I said. "I just happen to think it's a cooler place. Okay?"

"You are impossible!" Michel said. "We have seen the Mona Lisa —"

"Boring face, bad colors —"

"The Venus de Milo —"

"No arms! What a gyp."

"And all that incredible Etruscan pottery —"

"What's an Etrusc, anyway?"

The truth? The Louvre *was* great. Unbelievably awesome. But I couldn't admit that to Michel the Pest.

"I am leaving," Michel declared. "You are hopeless."

"Good riddance!"

He went to the left. I went to the right.

I saw a crowd in front of me. But not one familiar face. I walked farther and looked around the next corner.

Nothing.

I ran back to where I'd left Michel. Michel was wandering around, looking lost.

"Where's everybody else?" I asked.

"I was hoping you'd know," Michel said.

"Great, Michel. Just great. We're lost."

Michel glanced at his watch. "Let's go outside and wait for them."

"Which entrance? This place is humongous!" I thought for a moment. "I know! We came here by subway — Métro — whatever they call it. They'll have to go back to the station. We can wait there."

"Fine."

We ran out the nearest exit. The station was easy to find. It looks like a miniature museum itself.

We must have waited for an hour — *way* past the time the group was supposed to leave. Michel kept trying to make jokes, but I didn't say a word to him. I didn't even *look* at him.

Then I heard horrible screeching noises. I thought a cat was being tortured nearby.

I turned to see Michel playing his harmonica.

"What are you doing?" I said.

Clink! went a coin that someone had thrown to him.

Michel grinned. "If we stay here long enough, we can earn our own plane fare back."

"You think this is *funny*, don't you?" I said. "We are lost in a foreign city, Michel! Mr. D is probably calling the police. He's going to have to stop the tour. See what you've done? You've ruined this vacation for *everyone*!"

"Are you saying this is *my* fault?"

"Yes! If you hadn't distracted me in the museum, this wouldn't have happened!"

"You were provoking me!"

"I was not!"

"You were too!"

"Look," I said. "We're wasting time here. We have to do something."

Michel shrugged. "Wasn't there a Plan B, in case we got lost?"

I thought back to a little speech our chaperones had given us at the hotel. "Right," I said to Michel, "in case we separate from the group, we should meet at the Eiffel Tower at five o'clock. But that's four hours from now!"

Michel was marching straight for a pay phone. Before I could say anything, he was madly tapping out a number and speaking French to someone at the other end.

Then a second number and more French. "*C'est tout!*" he announced as he finally hung up. "I found out the number of the hotel. Then I called the hotel and left a message that you and I were going to follow Plan B."

"And what are we supposed to do until five o'clock?"

Michel grinned. "A beautiful day. Paris. Four hours of freedom. You. Me. We'll think of something."

Trapped. Tricked.

I couldn't go off by myself. I'm not stupid.

But there were other options. Just because we were *with* each other, we didn't have to be *together.*

First we went to a *patisserie,* which means pastry shop. "I don't know you," I said as we stood in line. "And we will sit at separate tables."

"Suit yourself." Michel turned away from me. He said something in French to the girl behind the counter, and she loaded up his plate. I was drooling just looking at it.

When it was my turn, I said, "I'll have what he had."

"Eh?" the girl said.

I pointed to the pastries behind the glass case. "This stuff. An assortment."

She shrugged and started speaking in rapid-fire French.

Meanwhile Michel was sitting by himself, stuffing his face.

Kristy

I walked over to him. I hated to have to ask for help, but I had no choice. "Will you translate for me?"

"Eh?" he replied. "Do I know you, young lady?"

The counter girl started laughing.

So did a few of the customers in line. Then some customers at the tables.

"Come, I will serve you," said the counter girl in perfect English.

A *prank*!

He had told her to pretend she didn't know English.

I was seeing red.

I have never felt so embarrassed in my life.

Who did he think he was?

Calmly I picked up a cream puff from Michel's plate. I gave it a good look.

Then I dropped it in his lap and headed for the door.

"Hey! Wait!" he shouted, following me out.

A few customers were applauding. Even that didn't make me feel better.

Michel caught up to me on the crowded sidewalk. He had a powdery white stain on his pants. But I wasn't laughing.

I could barely unclench my teeth to speak. *"Why did you do that to me?"*

"I'm sorry," Michel said. "Really. It was a stupid joke. I just — well, you said you didn't want to know me, and I guess that was a way to get you to sit next to me."

Bonk.

That response hit me over the head. It made absolutely no sense.

"But you — do you —" I sputtered. "You don't —"

Like me, I wanted to say. But it would have sounded idiotic. Michel hated me. He had to.

Still, he was looking at me with this sad, sorry expression. Was he faking? Was this another practical joke? I couldn't tell.

So I just turned and walked away.

"Wait! How are you going to communicate with the Parisians?" He was right behind me.

"Sign language. I don't know."

"But it's dangerous to be alone!" I could feel his hand touching my arm.

I whirled around. *"You're* dangerous. I don't trust you. *I don't like you. Now get lost before I scream!"*

As soon as the words left my mouth, I wanted to pull them back. I *was* screaming. People were staring at us.

Michel recoiled. That's the only way I can describe it. It was as if I'd hit him.

"I — I'm sorry," Michel said quietly. "I didn't

193

mean to hurt your feelings. I thought — you know, all our arguments, the insults — I thought we were just kidding around. I thought we were just having fun together. I wouldn't dream of hurting you, Kristy."

My head was spinning. I felt dizzy and angry and hurt and happy all at the same time. My arms were tense. My throat was tense.

I tried to look Michel in the eye. I tried to say something. But I couldn't.

Michel lowered his head. "Okay. Look. I could never forgive myself if something bad happened to you. My dad is French and I've been to Paris several times, so I can be useful to you, Kristy. Let's make a deal. We can *pretend* to be friends, like an acting exercise. I promise not to play pranks or make jokes. You promise not to insult me."

I am brave. I am strong. I can handle myself.

But I did not want to be alone. Not in a strange foreign city where people drive like maniacs and speak French.

Pretend?

He. Is. My. Friend, I said to myself.

This was not going to be easy. Not by a long shot.

I looked into his eyes. They were deep brown, like polished wood. I guess I hadn't really noticed them before.

He smiled. That made him look a little less revolting.

I figured I could stand it. For a few hours.

"Which way should we go?" I grumbled.

"The *Tuileries*?"

"Whatever."

We walked into this huge public garden, with flowers surrounded by low, trimmed hedges. Lots of kids were running around. They made me think of baby-sitting, and Stoneybrook. Both of which I was missing like crazy.

A little girl handed Michel a flower. Her mom scolded her, but Michel just smiled.

I smiled too. (Not at him. *With* him.)

One of the moms (or nannies, I couldn't tell) smiled and said something to Michel in French. He blushed.

"What?" I asked.

Michel shrugged. "She said we were a lovely couple."

I made a face. I took two long sidesteps away from him. Unfortunately, I nearly fell over a hedge.

Michel burst out laughing. So did the moms and nannies.

Part of me wanted to kick Michel. Part of me just wanted to run away. Part of me wanted to —

But I didn't. I started laughing too.

Kristy

"Let's get out of here," I said, brushing myself off.

Michel knew just where to go. I don't remember all the places — an ancient Egyptian monument, a palace that contained a science museum, an apartment-building-sized arch called *L'Arc de Triomphe* — but they were cool.

So was Michel. He was growing on me, I guess.

He even ordered for me when we visited another pastry shop.

"Thanks," I said between bites of croissant as we walked along this grand, tree-lined boulevard called the *Champs-Élysées* (pronounced something like *Shonz-ellie-zay*.)

Michel's face lit up. "A kind word! *Zut alors!*"

"Whatever," I replied. "It's good food."

"Are you saying this as yourself? Or is this still an acting exercise?" Michel asked, giving me this eager, puppy-dog look.

I let out a sudden laugh and nearly sprayed the *Champs-Élysées* with half-chewed croissant chunks. Which made me break into a coughing fit.

"Uh-oh." Michel darted behind me. He put his arms around my waist and started doing the Heimlich maneuver.

"Don't you dare!" I blurted out.

We were standing against an old brick build-

196

ing, near a public phone. I wasn't coughing anymore, but Michel still had me in a front-to-back hug. "Are you okay?"

"Fine." I smiled. A little. My acting was getting much better.

Michel seemed to notice where his arms were for the first time. He dropped them and began inching toward the phone. "Well. Uh, maybe I should call the hotel? In case the group has returned."

Quickly he picked up the receiver and made a call. When he returned, he was grinning. "Mr. D left a message saying he's gotten *our* message. He'll meet us at the Eiffel Tower at five."

I glanced at my watch. "It's only four."

"A walk by the River Seine, *ma chérie*?" Michel held out his arm, like someone in an old movie.

It was goony. But hey, we were acting, right? Besides, I love rivers. They are so peaceful.

I took his arm. "*Sí*," I said.

"*Oui*," he corrected me.

Arm in arm, we walked along the river to the Eiffel Tower. And soon I forgot that Michel was Michel and I was me.

I guess we had sort of *become* our characters.

As we rode up the crowded elevator of the tower, my character felt tired. So she rested her head against Michel's character's shoulder.

More people were smiling at us. A woman actually called us a "cute pair" — in English.

Oh, well. She was entitled to her opinion.

As we strolled out onto the observation deck, the traffic noise seemed far away. The city stretched out below us, on either side of the Seine. I thought I detected a faint bakery scent on the warm summer breeze.

"They're here," Michel said softly.

I looked straight down. A tour bus was pulling up to the curb.

"End of acting exercise, huh?" I said.

"We have a few more minutes."

Michel put his arm around my shoulder.

I let it stay there. My character didn't mind it at all.

Mr. Dougherty was waiting for us anxiously as we emerged from the elevator.

"Are you all right?" he asked.

"Fine," Michel and I said at the same time.

As we approached the bus, Abby, Stacey, Jessi, Mal, and a few Berger students came running off.

Michel went off with his friends. I had a big hugfest with mine.

Stacey was giving me a sly grin. "So, how was it?"

I shrugged. "I'm a big girl. I can handle being lost."

Kristy

"Yeah, but lost with the guy you absolutely *hate* the most?" Abby asked. "That must have been *awful*."

They were teasing me.

But I didn't care.

I just smiled. "Hey, I'm a good actress."

CHAPTER 20

Mary Anne

Monday

I'm just getting used to Playground Camp.

I'm getting used to Buddy Barrett's crazy antics.

I'm getting used to the freeze-tag games in which kids try to crack each other up with their poses.

And I'm definitely getting used to working side by side with Dawn.

There's only one thing I can't get used to....

Mary Anne

"Okay, guys, Ms. Garcia called to say she'll be late," Jerry announced. "That means I'm in charge. So wake up — ten minutes till the kids are here! I need two volunteers for softball!"

"Me," Logan called out.

I raised my hand.

"Me too!" Cokie piped up.

"Okay . . . Logan, Cokie," Jerry said, writing the names on his pad. "Playground monitors?"

Cokie was grinning at me. As if she'd won something.

I was so, so sick of her behavior. She was ruining the camp experience for me.

"Excuse me, Jerry," Janine said. "Mary Anne had her hand up."

"Hand?" Jerry repeated. "Uh, Janine, this isn't an honors classroom. You have to yell to get what you want. Playground monitors?"

Janine had been sitting at the picnic bench. Now she stood up. "What did you say?"

Jerry gave her a weary look. "'Playground mon —'"

"No. Before that. The comment about an honors classroom. That was unfair and insulting."

Whoosh. Away flew my thoughts about Cokie.

I could not believe this was Janine talking. I looked at Claudia. Her jaw was open in shock.

"Can this wait, Janine?" Jerry said. "We now have eight and a half minutes."

"No," Janine said firmly. "I was pointing out that Cokie had railroaded Mary Anne. Listening to me would have taken very little time. By verbally abusing me, *you* are causing this argument. Therefore, *you* are wasting time."

"Go, girl!" Claudia shouted.

"Well — why —" Jerry sputtered. "Okay, fine. Mary Anne, you do softball."

"Hey, that's unfair!" Cokie yelped.

"Cokie, you hate softball," Bruce Schermerhorn said.

Cokie glared at me. "Mary Anne hates it even worse. She was just volunteering so she could be with *Logan*. Weren't you, Mary Anne?"

"Well, I —" I *hate* confrontation. Especially when other people are around. I wanted to crumple up and cry.

This was supposed to be fun. This was my summer *vacation*.

"Don't listen to her, Mary Anne," Claudia said. "Cokie, you are *so* out of line."

"Can we please get started?" Jerry asked. "Cokie, you and Dawn do playground duty —"

"No," I blurted out.

I couldn't take this.

Cokie had been right. Yes, I do hate softball.

203

MaryAnne

And yes, I was volunteering just to be near Logan. Well, and to keep Cokie away from Logan.

But that was the problem. Her behavior was forcing me to make decisions. I wasn't free to think for myself.

Which was just plain wrong.

"Cokie can coach softball," I said.

Logan was slashing the air horizontally with downturned palms, as if to say *No!*

Cokie smiled triumphantly. Then she turned and saw Logan.

Her face fell. "Oh," she said dully. "I can see I'm not wanted."

"Will you guys please grow up?" Jerry pleaded.

"My feelings exactly," Cokie said, storming away. "I hate being around babies. I quit."

"Come back here!" Jerry yelled.

"Oh, stuff it, Michaels," Cokie replied.

Jerry threw down his clipboard. "Terrific. I'm losing a counselor. You see what you started, Janine?"

Janine's eyes widened. I thought she was going to cry.

She took a deep breath. She looked straight at Jerry and said, "Stuff it, Michaels."

Claudia let out a hoot.

I almost did too.

Janine turned away and jogged after Cokie, stopping her by the playground entrance. Janine talked to her calmly, with a concerned, respectful expression.

Jerry's face looked ashen. "Well, uh, let's get to work."

Logan smiled at me. I smiled back.

He and Bruce Schermerhorn ran to the equipment shed.

Dawn and I went to the playground. "This is the most exciting day so far," she said, "and the kids aren't even here yet."

Out of the corner of my eye, I saw Janine and Cokie greeting the Barrett/DeWitt kids as they came in.

Cokie took Taylor DeWitt's hand, and they skipped over to the hopscotch area.

Janine was beaming. "Jerry?" she called out. "The gate hinge is coming loose. Can you find a screwdriver?"

Jerry muttered something and walked inside.

I could see a tiny smile forming on Janine's face.

Claudia ran to her from the arts and crafts area, gave her a big kiss, and ran back.

I was very impressed.

CHAPTER 21

Mallory

Monday

Big day. Visiting lots of sights.

Am really making progress on my new story. Will show you when I get home.

Writer's Journal

Mariel ~~yessed in her sheets~~ tossed and turned. Something was off. Could it have been the milk she had drunk ~~the~~ ~~last~~ night before? It ~~did~~ had tasted ~~funny~~ a bit sour. But that wouldn't explain the strange, coarse feel of the sheets. And the ~~strong~~ vague odor of old wood and candle wax.

But it was the loud, rhythmic clop-clop-clop outside her window that finally ~~jolted~~ made her eyes spring open.

206

"Earth to Mal!" Jessi said.

I quickly closed my journal and looked up.

The park benches around me were empty. A moment ago, they'd been full of SMS and Berger students.

"Where is everybody?" I asked.

Jessi was standing over me, hands on hips. "Walking through the Tuileries. Admiring the flowers. Which is what we're supposed to be doing."

I stood up, tucking my journal under my arm. "Sorry. I was at the good part."

"Yeah? Is Mariel in the past yet?"

"She just made the time switch. But she doesn't know it yet."

We were approaching the group now. Everyone was oohing and aahing over flowers.

"Kristy was right," Jessi said. "This place is stunning."

"Do you think she should let anyone know?" I asked.

"Who? Kristy? She *did* —"

"No, Mariel. I mean, if someone else *knew*, then that might add extra suspense to the plot. You know, will the trusted person reveal the secret? Or do you think that would take the emphasis away from Mariel's inner thoughts?"

"Mallory?" Jessi said. "Can I ask you a question?"

"Sure."

"Do you remember where we've been today?"

"Um." I was drawing a blank. "Wait. That big jail place —"

Jessi laughed. "The *Bastille*! Did you hear what the guide said? You know, that the French Revolution started there, after six hundred people stormed it and released all the prisoners?"

"Cool," I said. "I missed that part. I must have been writing."

"You were writing at the Cathedral of Notre Dame too."

"I know, but that was the toughest part. I had to straighten out all the details about Mariel's life in the present."

"That place was *incredible*, Mallory! It's eight hundred years old. It took two hundred years to build. The frescoes, the statues, the flying buttresses —"

I burst out laughing. "The *what*?"

"Girl, have you forgotten something? We are in *Paris*. You may never have a chance to see this place again."

"As soon as I finish the story —"

"Look, I know I'm not a writer, okay? But

when I was in the Bastille, I thought of a dozen story ideas."

"Then you should carry a notebook. Writers need to write all the time."

"And dancers need to dance, Mal. But we also have to rest. We have to experience life. If you spend all your time writing, you're forgetting to live. And if you forget to live, how can you be a good writer?"

Hmmm.

I hadn't looked at it that way.

I glanced at my notebook again.

I knew what I needed to write. The ideas weren't going to fly away.

"Okay," I said, tucking my notebook into my backpack. "I guess Mariel can wait until Stoneybrook."

Well, I am really glad I listened to Jessi. I loved our visit to the Latin Quarter. We wandered through the Sorbonne (an ancient French university that's still active), and Mr. D somehow found this weird little museum in a police station that featured torture weapons and displays of Paris's most grisly crimes. (I thought I was going to barf. Jessi said, "This'll be perfect for your first horror novel.") But my favorite part of the day was eating dinner in a cozy little bistro with brick walls and a working fireplace.

I was stuffed and happy when we reached our hotel.

Jessi fell asleep right away. But I couldn't.

So I turned on my night-light. And I took out my journal.

Okay, so we weren't in Stoneybrook yet.

I was only doing it to make myself tired. That's all.

The sunlight blinded her. Through squint~~y~~ed eyes she made out the shape of ~~pretty~~ gauzy, waving fabric. White fabric. Not at all like the curtains over her bed.

She sat up and looked out the window. And what she saw nearly made her heart stop. No ~~house~~ driveway, no maple trees, no familiar sight of the Timmermans' house across the street. In fact, there was no paved street at all.

<u>I have a feeling I'm not in Stoney field anymore</u>, Mariel said to herself. . . .

Abby

Monday

Our last full day.
Sob, sob, sob.
Actually, I'm looking
forward to going home.
I've had enough.
Once you've stepped
on royalty, nothing
else quite measures up.
Besides, Elvismania
is dead in Paris.
Okay. Travelogue.
Today we visited an
inside-out building.
It's called the Centre
Georges Pompidou.

All the pipes and tubes, and hoses and elevators are on the exterior, painted bright colors. Inside is an art museum.

Kristy and I spent most of the time riding the glass elevator up and down and looking at the performers in the plaza below us. I don't even remember the art.

This afternoon, some kids are going to Euro Disney. Not me, though.

My Paris roommate, Kristy, and I are going to spend our final, romantic Parisian hours in the sewer....

"**W**hat's the point of being in *Paris* and going to Disneyland?" grumbled Kristy.

"Right," I said.

"You can go there anytime when you're in the States."

"Yup."

"But you can only take a tour of the Paris sewer system when you're in Paris."

"Exactly."

I've learned not to disagree with Kristy when she's in a mood. I wasn't sure *why* she was grumpy, but I wasn't asking.

Besides, I really was thrilled about this tour. I mean, think about it. How can you really *know* a city without seeing what's underneath it?

Most of the other SMS and Berger kids were piling into the EuroDisney tour bus. Stacey was helping her mom round up the Stoneybrook gang. It was nice to see the two McGills getting along again. That trip to Normandy really seemed to bring them together.

"Hey! Are you sure you don't want to come?"

That was Michel. Shouting out the bus window.

Kristy rolled her eyes. "Are you sure you *want* to?"

Hmmm. I wasn't expecting her to say *that*.

"Ahhh, so *that's* the problem," I said. "Despair not, fair Kristy. The man of your dreams shall return to your arms, loaded down with Goofy souvenirs."

"Ha-ha, Abby, *so* funny," Kristy said, grumping back into the hotel.

I followed her, because I hadn't done my after-breakfast tooth-brushing. (I'm sure the sewers smelled bad enough without my morning monster mouth.)

Soon we were again outside with our little group of sewer seekers. Mr. D led us to the métro, which we took to the *Pont-de-l'Alma* station.

It was a gorgeous day. I figured we'd be the only ones crazy enough to be in the sewers (or *égouts*, as the Parisians say). Well, guess what? The place was packed.

I couldn't stop cracking up. The image of these nicely dressed, old tourists crawling around in the slimy pipes was too funny.

"Ssshh," said Kristy the Grouch.

Well, it turns out these sewers are a major deal. In fact, before you take the tour, you have to see a movie about them. Fact: They are eighteen feet high by fourteen feet wide. Fact: There are over thirteen hundred miles of sewer in Paris! Fact: *Boats* used to go through them. Fact: Not anymore. We had to walk.

Shhhhhwwippp, went my sinuses as soon as we descended. Closed up tight.

Abby

Mold, I guess. Or rotten food. Or dust. I won't go any further.

"I wish Ballory were here," I said. "She could thick of all kides of good stories."

"Some people don't know what they're missing," Kristy muttered.

"AHHHHHHH-CHOOOOOOO!" I sneezed.

"A H H H H H H H -C H O O O O O O O! CHOOOOOOO! CHOOOOOOO!" answered my sewer echo voice.

"Abby, ssshh!" Kristy said.

"It was a sdeeze! I could't help it!"

Lots of kids started imitating me. The tunnel was resounding with sneezes, shouts, and giggles.

I thought it was pretty funny. Kristy looked as if she didn't want to know me.

"What's wrogg with you, Kristy?" I said. "This is supposed to be fud!"

"I'm fine," Kristy snapped.

"*I* doe what's botherigg you." I dug out a spray decongestant from my pack and took a couple of inhalations. Right away my sinuses began to clear. "You're pinigg away for your far-flugg lover-boy."

Okay, it was a stupid thing to say. But it was a joke.

Well, Kristy didn't take it that way.

She recoiled from me like a slingshot. "You have to broadcast it to everyone, don't you?"

"Huh? I was just —"

"As if I don't need any privacy —"

"Privacy? In the *sewer*?"

"You know what I mean!"

"Kristy, look, I didn't mean to start a fight."

"Then why did you bring it up?"

"Bring *what* up?"

"I can't help it, okay?"

"Wait. I'm lost here. Can we start this conversation over?"

"I didn't mean to. I hated him! And then I didn't. It just . . . happened."

"Ahhh."

I was beginning to understand.

Unfortunately, so was the entire Paris sewer system. Everyone was staring at us.

"Ahem," said our guide. "Years ago, the sewers became an accessory to an infamous crime. . . ."

"Are you serious, Kristy?" I whispered.

"That's what I've been asking myself!" Kristy replied.

"Does he like you back?"

"I think so. Maybe not. I don't know!"

"He seems to."

"He just acts that way to annoy me."

Abby

"So what'll you do about this?"

"Nothing!"

"And stay miserable?"

"I'm not miserable!"

"Could have fooled me."

". . . The bank robbers used their knowledge of the underworld, so to speak," the guide droned on, "and they made their getaway through these tunnels. . . ."

"What else *can* I do?" Kristy said.

"Tell him, of course!"

"And make a fool of myself?"

"How else are you going to find out how he feels?"

"Okay. Say he does like me. So what? He goes home. I go home. End of story."

"Canada's not that far away from Connecticut. Look. At the party tonight, when everyone's feeling good and loose, just go somewhere with him. A dark corner, whatever. Tell him how you feel, and see what happens. What have you got to lose?"

"No way."

"You are so *stubborn*! Okay, Kristy. If you don't talk to him, I will."

"You wouldn't!"

"I shouldn't have to."

The tour had moved on, and Mr. D was calling us.

Kristy began walking toward him. "Okay, okay."

"You will?" I asked.

"I was talking to Mr. D."

"What about tonight?"

"I'll *think* about it."

"Good!"

I didn't believe her for a minute.

CHAPTER 23

Kristy

Monday

And that wraps it up. Tomorrow we head back to good old Stoneybrook.

Right now everybody's at a big going-home party downstairs. Not me, though. I'm beat.

I'm sure Abby, Stacey, Jessi, and Mal will have plenty to report.

Good night. . . .

I lied.

Sort of.

I did try to go to sleep. But it didn't work. (Anyway, I was lying in bed fully clothed.)

Each time I closed my eyes, I'd see a coop full of chickens, running around and clucking.

That's what I felt like. A chicken.

Michel was a boy.

And even though he was hateful, I sort of liked him.

That's all.

I mean, I've had boy friends *and* a boyfriend. No big whoop.

So why was I making this into such a big deal? All I had to do was *talk* to him. I'm good at talking.

Maybe I needed practice.

I turned the light on and looked in the mirror. I pushed my hair out of my face.

"Hi, Michel," I said. "Remember the Eiffel Tower? That was cool, wasn't it?"

Dumb.

"You know, you're not as creepy as I thought."

No way.

"Yo, DuMoulin. Want to have a . . ."

A what? A relationship? I hate that word.

This was ridiculous.

I had to do it. Just go down there and do it.

If he laughed at me, I could always pitch a stuffed mushroom at him.

I tucked in my T-shirt. I straightened my Mets cap. And I yanked open my door.

I came face-to-face with a clenched fist.

"Oh! Sorry! I was just about to knock!" Michel said, quickly letting his arm drop.

"What are you doing up here?" I asked.

"What are *you* doing up here? Everyone's at the party."

"I was about to go."

He smiled. "But I'm here."

"Good. I'll go. You stay."

Michel strolled inside. "You trust me alone in a room full of Mets souvenirs and an open window?"

"Even *you* wouldn't be low enough to do that," I said, closing the door behind us.

Michel was sliding open my glass door, stepping onto the balcony. "Nice night," he said.

We leaned over the railing. The night air had a faint flowery smell mixed with the pollution. The streetlights threaded their way through the city below, disappearing behind darkened office buildings. To our left, the Eiffel Tower glowed brightly.

"You can see it from just about anywhere in Paris," Michel remarked.

"Yeah," I said. "It almost looks like it was constructed out of light, not steel."

I leaned against him.

He put his arm around my shoulders.

His face was near mine. I mean, really close.

He seemed to have finished talking. And I knew *I* had nothing else to say.

So I kissed him.

It was no big deal. No violins and fireworks.

It seemed like the logical thing to do.

We stood there for a long time, looking over Paris. Neither of us said much. I never did what Abby wanted me to do. I never told him how I felt.

But that was okay.

I didn't have to.

He knew.

I was up early the next morning. Abby was still snoring when I left the room.

The Berger kids had to leave earlier than we did. The first one I saw was Darcy Boynton. I told her that Abby was conked out, but that I'd force her to write.

I almost didn't see Michel, stepping onto the bus.

"Yo! DuMoulin!" I called out.

He smiled and hopped off the bus. "Thomas! Hey. Well, time to go, eh?"

"Yeah."

I wasn't going to make a big mushy scene in front of everybody. That's not my style.

But he hugged me, so I hugged him back.

"Keep in touch," he said. "And come to Toronto some time."

"You come to Stoneybrook too," I suggested. "Hey, do you baby-sit?"

"Do I *what*?"

"Never mind."

I let him kiss me. On the cheek.

He climbed onto the bus again.

I stood there while the others boarded.

When the bus pulled away, I waved.

I think Michel waved back. The windows were tinted, so it was hard to tell.

I felt this heaviness in my chest as I went back to my room. My eyes were watery.

Weird.

I never feel that way so early in the morning.

I must have been really, really tired.

Or something.

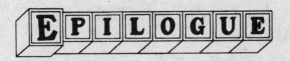

EPILOGUE

Dear Kristy,

Haven't heard from you. Well, I haven't written either. So what are you complaining about?

Just kidding. Anyway, Toronto's hot. I've spent most of the week in my air-conditioned living room, watching the Blue Jays rise to the TOP OF THEIR DIVISION.

Sorry. You know how I hate bragging.

How are you? Coming up to Toronto soon? Ever been to a WORLD SERIES GAME in Canada? It's fun, even if your favorite team's not good enough to qualify.

There I go again. Apologies.

Anyway, that's about it. Write back.

and don't take the Mets' season
too hard.
There's always next year.

Remember Paris!
Michel

Dear Mallory,
I enclose for your perusal this advance
notice, from the <u>Orton Family Review of
Books</u>:
Upon reading the first, lushly illustrated
pages of <u>An Accident of Time</u>, by Mallory
Pike, we are struck by the rich, skillfully
depicted characters. As if that weren't
pleasure enough, we soon find ourselves
surrendering with delight to the
intriguing premise. As the plot gallops
along, our hearts open to the heroine,
Mariel, and we despair that any writer
could possibly have the skill to resolve
our heroine's dilemma satisfactorily.
Luckily, Mallory Pike accomplishes
this and much more. It is a smashing
debut, and we look forward to future
works from this gifted young author.
<u>Brava</u>, Mallory! You have the family
gift.
Your cousin and number-one fan,
Gillian

226

P.S. I <u>LOVED</u> it too!!!!!!! ~~Kids~~
Write more!!!
             Cinserely,
             Bernard

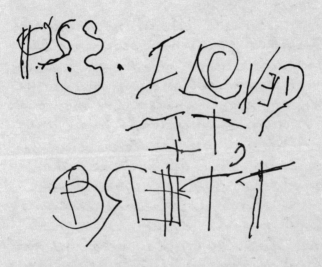

(That means Brett liked it too.
His writing stinks.
             —Bernard)

Louis P. Anderson
32471 Forest Canyon Drive
Parker, CO

Dear Stacey,

I don't think I properly thanked you and your mother for your good deed in France.

I am sitting in my home office, surrounded by memories. Photos of my wife and my children, my college buddies, Dennis, and of course, the photo I took of you two.

I had a strange dream last night. Now, I'm not one for heavy psychology and I sure feel a little funny writing this, but I thought you and your mom would understand. In my dream, Dennis is young again. He's in his navy uniform and he's heading out to sea alone on a forty-foot sailboat. I yell for him to come to shore, but he shakes his head and says, "I'm exactly where I want to be!"

And he disappears over the
horizon.

Well, take it for what it
is, a crazy dream from an
old man. But I want you to

know, Stacey, that at my age
I can think back over a
lot of extraordinary
kindnesses given to me over
my life — and what you and
your mom did stands out
among them all. I will
never forget it.

Yours truly,
Louis Anderson

DANCE NY

Dearest Jessica!
I know I can't
have you in my
permanent company
yet.
How about a
compromise?
Would you dance
in our Production
of the Nutcracker?

*Let me know
A.S.A.P.
We can work
out a weekend
rehearsal schedule.
Best to your parents.
— David Brailsford*

Dear Abby,
        Seeing you this month was THE
BOMBEST BOMB! Can you come
again? How about Decembre? I
will be meating the Queen again,
at another gayla. If you rite me
back with your news, I will pass
it on to her, as I am sure she
is dieing to hear.
        Oh. Inclosed is something I
know you'll want to see. Its
from the weekly newsmagazine.
It came out just after you left.
        You see, your FAMOUS!

VICTORIA

Hi, Katheryn!

Remember me? Jessi from Stoney-brook? Well, guess what? I may be dancing in NYC — in a <u>Nutcracker</u>!

Just mentioning it. I don't know for sure yet. I was invited, but my parents don't seem too thrilled.

I'll work on them. And I'll let you know.

How far is Toronto from New York?

Yours,
Jessi

Michel —
            BLUE JAYS STINK!!!!!
            LET'S GO, METS!!!!

                            — Kristy

P.S. A World Series in Canada? Get
      real. Not this year.
P.P.S. What's Toronto like in October?
      Around the time of Columbus
      Day weekend. Or do you know
      who Columbus was?
            Just asking.
P.P.P.S. You better write back.
P.P.P.P.S. Or else.

Ann M. Martin

About the Author

ANN MATTHEWS MARTIN was born on August 12, 1955. She grew up in Princeton, NJ, with her parents and her younger sister, Jane.

Although Ann used to be a teacher and then an editor of children's books, she's now a full-time writer. She gets ideas for her books from many different places. Some are based on personal experiences. Others are based on childhood memories and feelings. Many are written about contemporary problems or events.

All of Ann's characters, even the members of the Baby-sitters Club, are made up. (So is Stoneybrook.) But many of her characters are based on real people. Sometimes Ann names her characters after people she knows, other times she chooses names she likes.

In addition to the Baby-sitters Club books, Ann Martin has written many other books for children. Her favorite is *Ten Kids, No Pets* because she loves big families and she loves animals. Her favorite Baby-Sitters Club book is *Kristy's Big Day*. (By the way, Kristy is her favorite baby-sitter!)

Ann M. Martin now lives in New York with her cats, Gussie, Woody, and Willy. Her hobbies are reading, sewing, and needlework — especially making clothes for children.